AF228036

MISSING

By

Cheryl Russell

Copyright © 2019 Cheryl Russell

The moral right of the author has been asserted. Apart from any fair dealing for the purposes of research or private study, or criticism or review, as permitted under the Copyright, Designs and patent Act 1988, this publication may only be reproduced, stored or transmitted in any form or by any means, with the prior permission in writing of the publishers, or in the case or reprographic reproduction in accordance with the terms of licences issued by the Copyright Licensing Agency. Enquiries concerning reproduction outside those terms should be sent to the publishers.

This is a work of fiction. Names, characters, businesses, places, events and incidents are either the products of the author's imagination or used in a fictitious manner. Any resemblance to actual persons, living or dead, or actual events is purely coincidental.

Other books by this author

Lily of the Valley

The Necklace

Evening Treats a collection of short stories

The One Who Got Away

Murderous Feet

Gallows Lane

A Bruised Reed

Chapter One

The phone rang, bringing Mary out of a deep sleep. She leaned her arm over to the bedside cabinet and picked up the phone. "Hello," she said in a sleepy voice.

She froze as she listened to a robotic voice speaking, "Follow. All. Instructions. In. This. Call. Or. You'll. Never. See. Your. Daughter. Again."

Wide awake now she got out of bed and rushed to her daughter's room. Not wanting to wake her she opened the door slowly to avoid the squeak it often made. She crept over to the bed, satisfying herself that there was someone there. The duvet was lifted up and the pillows covered as usual. This was how her daughter, Bethany liked to sleep, cuddling her favourite soft toy Piglet. She left the room shaking her head and disconnected the call. It must be a prank call especially at that time of night. She settled back into bed with a smile as she thought of her six year old daughter. She was a feisty, intelligent, extrovert who loved playing with friends. She was well ahead of the rest of the class in reading and maths. She often complained of being bored at school. She was very quick to pick up new things. She was really flourishing. Even at such a young age Mary had high hopes for Bethany's future.

In the morning, Mary was awoken by her alarm going off. She groaned wishing she could have more sleep. It had been such a broken night with that prank call. She got up and went straight to Bethany to get her up for school. It was unusual for Bethany not to be awake and climbing all over Mary when the alarm went off. The bed looked as it had when she had gone in during the night. She smiled to herself. Her daughter was still very much in dreamland, it was a shame to have to disturb her. She pulled the duvet back, saying, "Come on sleepy……" She stopped abruptly. The bed was empty with just a pillow stuffed down making it look as if there was someone in the bed.

Mary sank to her knees, burying her head in her hands, "Oh my God, what have I done."

She stayed there for what seemed like hours but was in fact only a few minutes before getting up and going to look at her phone. Maybe she would be able to find out a number that made the call during the night. Private number! Now what was she to do? What had happened to her beautiful daughter? Was she still alive? Would she see her again? If only she had taken more notice during the night, maybe information would have been given to get her daughter back or some detail as to who had taken her.

She was sat on the side of the bed trying to think. She thought about calling her ex husband, but they hadn't been in touch in six months when she had finally come to her senses and thrown him out. She assumed he was living with one of his many girlfriends.

Bethany had kept asking about daddy but Mary successfully changed the subject every time and Bethany had finally stopped asking.

Mary looked up Jez's number and dialled before she could change her mind. She didn't know what else to do.

"Yes," asked Jez.

"Thank God you're there. It's Bethany, she's disappeared. I woke up this morning to find her gone."

"What do you mean gone?"

"Disappeared. She's not in bed."

"Did she get up and go downstairs?"

Mary didn't respond, feeling very silly. How could she not have thought of that herself? That must be it, Bethany was just playing hide and seek.

"You haven't checked. Next time don't call unless it's a matter of life or death. It was you who threw me out remember. It's up to you to stand on your own two feet and not come running to me at every problem." He disconnected the call.

Mary stared at the phone.

"Bethany," she called as she put a dressing gown on and went downstairs. There was no answer.

"Come on Bethany, stop hiding, it's not funny. Mummy's getting worried."

She looked around expecting Bethany to jump out from behind the sofa shouting "Boo!"

Silence! A thorough search confirmed than Bethany wasn't in the house.

She tried Jez again but got no answer. She left a voicemail to let him know Bethany wasn't there. A few minutes later her phone went ping to let her know she'd got a message. It was Jez: *Don't bother me again. It's not my problem.*

How could he be so callous? This was his daughter, but it seemed as if he'd washed his hands of her.

What could she do? She had to do something. She decided to ring her best friend Liz. "Can you ring back later, I'm busy getting Tim ready for school."

"Please don't hang up," said Mary, pleading with her friend.

Liz detecting Mary was close to tears said, "What's happened?"

"It's Bethany, she isn't here."

"What do you mean she isn't there?"

"I've searched the house from top to bottom but there's no sign of her."

"Try and stay calm. I'll pop in when I've dropped Tim at school."

"Thank you! Thank you! I really appreciate it."

Mary supposed she should have a shower and get dressed but couldn't be bothered. All she could think about was her daughter. What if Bethany were to ring the bell while she was in the shower? She had a sudden thought, rushing into her daughter's bedroom she checked. Piglet was still on the bed. Bethany wouldn't sleep without Piglet. How could he have been left behind. It was a disaster. Bethany would never go anywhere without her favourite soft toy.

The doorbell went. Mary rushed downstairs hoping whoever had taken her daughter had second thoughts and had brought her back.

"Oh it's you," said Mary flatly.

"Who else were you expecting?" asked Liz.

"I thought maybe it was someone bringing Bethany back."

"You still haven't found her."

Mary shook her head letting the tears fall. Liz took her friend in her arms and held her while she cried.

"What have you done so far?" queried Liz when Mary was quieter.

"Phoned Jez and searched the house."

"Jez? I can't believe he would have been interested." Liz had always had a low opinion of him.

"He wasn't."

"I'm not surprised. He never has shown much interest in Bethany."

"I know," sighed Mary. "But I thought he'd show more interest knowing his daughter was missing, but you're right, he didn't care."

"How about phoning the police."

"I hadn't thought of that."

"That's the first thing you should have done."

"I suppose you're right but I'm not exactly thinking straight."

"I'm not surprised. Neither would I be if it were me."

Mary continued sitting there making no attempt to reach for the phone to make the call.

"Would you like me to do it?" asked Liz.

Mary nodded.

"They're sending someone round," said Liz, putting the phone back on the coffee table. "How about you going to have a shower and get dressed. I'll be here if there's a phone call or the doorbell."

Mary shook her head. She didn't want to miss anything not for a single second. She couldn't bear it to be Liz who let Bethany in if she were to appear. She was sure if her daughter were to turn up she would hug her to death. She wouldn't let go. It was losing her like this that made Mary realise how much she loved her Bethany. Being a single mum was hard going but she got by. Sometimes wishing she had someone to share the responsibility with or to give her a much needed break from Bethany's endless chatter. How she longed to hear her little chatterbox. Mary didn't know where she got it from as both she and her ex were quiet, introverted people. Bethany would chatter to anyone.

Mary wondered if she was chatting away to her kidnapper and driving him mad. Somehow the thought made her smile.

"What are you smiling about?" asked Liz.

"I was just wondering if miss chatterbox is driving the kidnapper mad with all her talking."

Even Liz smiled at this thought, although at first she had been disapproving of her friend's smile in the face of tragedy.

"Maybe he'll be so fed up he'll bring her back. He'll realise his mistake."

Liz had other thoughts in her mind but didn't want to share with Mary as it would make her worry even more. If it helped her friend to be light hearted, even flippant then that was a good thing. Liz was more inclined to think Bethany might be unconscious to keep her quiet. Whoever had taken her wouldn't want her giving away where she was.

………

The doorbell rang. Mary stood up rushing to the door hoping….. she was disappointed to see two uniformed officers standing there and not her daughter. She had been so ready to pull Bethany close and never let go.

Mary just stood there looking at the officers.

"Can we come in?" asked the taller of the two.

Mary nodded but didn't say a word. She moved aside to let them pass.

They nodded at Liz and then introduced themselves. "Hello we are PC Jones and WPC Witts."

"I'm Mary and this is my friend Liz. Please take a seat."

They all sat down in silence. The officers were taking the opportunity to have a look around the room. They always felt it gave them a feel of the family and how close they might be. Sometimes they would find a subtle clue as to what might have happened. In this case they noted the absence of any male figure in the photos on the mantlepiece.

"Your husband? Where is he?"

"We're separated," said Mary, somewhat bitterly.

"Ok. We'll need his contact details at some point as we'll have to talk to him," said WPC Witts, taking the lead.

"He won't want to know. I've already called him. The first time he suggested I look around the house before panicking as he was sure she must have come down by herself. The second time I phoned to say she wasn't anywhere he didn't answer his phone.

I left a message and he texted me back to say not to bother him, he didn't want to know. He suggested it was my fault for throwing him out. What was I supposed to do he was regularly cheating on me. I'd find out about one woman then he'd say he'd dropped her but then it would be some other floozy." Mary shut up, wondering if she'd said too much.

The officers were both taking notes. "That's helpful, but we'll still need to talk to him," said WPC Witts.

PC Jones just nodded. They had decided on the way that it would be Witts who would take the lead as she would be the family liaison officer.

"And where do you fit into this madam?" queried Jones looking at Liz.

"I'm Mary's best friend. She called me when she got rebuffed by Jez. It was me who said she should phone you."

"Quite right to," said Witts. "Why didn't you phone us first?" continued Witts.

"I was in a panic, I couldn't even think what I was supposed to do."

The officers both nodded. Panic did strange things to people making them unable to think clearly about the way forward.

"Well we're here now so tell us everything you can. When did you last see Bethany?"

"When I put her to bed."

"And what time would that be?"

"About 6.30pm."

"You didn't get up to her in the night?"

"No she usually slept through."

"Mary that's not strictly true, you have to tell them about the phone call," said Liz.

"What phone call?" asked Witts, looking from one woman to the other, suddenly alert.

"I was woken up in the night by the phone ringing."

There was silence. Mary didn't say anything further until prompted to do so by Jones.

"It sounded like a robotic voice saying I wouldn't see my daughter again if I didn't follow instructions. I immediately got out of bed and went to check on Bethany. I found the duvet all humped up and the pillow half way down the bed which was the way Bethany slept. I assumed she must be there and not wanting to wake her I crept back to my room, disconnecting the call, thinking it was just someone's idea of a joke."

She paused.

"Carry on. What happened next?" asked Jones.

"I went back to sleep and woke when my alarm went off. I was surprised as Bethany usually comes in to my room climbing all over me to wake me up before the alarm goes off. Today she didn't. I went to her room and found the duvet and pillow in the same position. Thinking she must have been very tired to sleep this long I opened the curtains and went to the bed pulling the duvet back. I was horrified to discover the bed empty." Mary began to cry. Liz put her arm around Mary's shoulders in an effort to comfort her friend. There was no way of taking the pain away.

"That's when you phoned your ex?" queried Witts.

Mary nodded.

"Was there anything about that voice on the phone that sounded familiar?"

Mary shook her head. "It just sounded like a robot might speak."

"Were there any background noises that might identify where the call was made."

"I didn't take any notice, sorry."

"That's ok. It was the middle of the night so you would have been half asleep anyway."

"Well, we'll put out a call for all officers to keep an eye out for a little girl. Can you describe what she was wearing for us when you last saw her?"

Straightaway Mary pictured Bethany in her mind with her favourite pyjamas. "They were blue pyjamas with little ballerinas in pink. She loves ballet you see."

"Thanks that helps. We'll be off now and interview Jez to see what he can tell us. I'll be back later to update you," said WPC Witts, before continuing, "I will be your liaison officer. This means I'm the point of contact between you and the police. I'll be updating you on the investigation and supporting you at this difficult time. If you think of anything else we might need to know you just have to get in touch with me."

The two officers stood up and PC Jones took the piece of paper with Jez's contact details from Mary and they left.

Liz turned to Mary after they had gone and put her arm around her friend who was in tears.

"It's going to be ok. They'll find her you'll see. Maybe she'll even be back by bedtime tonight."

"But what if she's not. I might never see her again and I can't cope with it." Mary broke into a fresh bout of sobbing. Liz held her tight without speaking.

"I'll put the kettle on and make you a nice cup of tea."

Mary shook her head, feeling if she were to eat or drink she would bring it straight back up again.

"Ok, but you must eat and drink at some point soon or you'll be ill yourself then what use will you be to Bethany when you get her back."

"My baby! Gone!"

"The police will find her. You'll be reunited soon you'll see."

Chapter Two

"What did you make of Mary?" asked Jones when the two officers were back in the car and driving away to see Jez.

"I'm not sure, I'm puzzled why she only appears to make a cursory glance to see if Bethany was in bed instead of looking closely. She says she didn't want to wake her up but if it were me I would want to be absolutely sure. I think I'd want to hold on to her and never let go. Also the robotic sounding voice is a bit strange. How could that have been accomplished. I know people disguise their voice if they don't want to be identified but robotic sounds a bit far fetched, as if we are in the middle of a sci fi book."

"I agree it does sound a bit odd. It might just be the way it came across to her of course and that was the best way to describe it. Maybe you need to question her further about the voice."

WPC Witts nodded in affirmation.

"Of course if it were a robotic voice or otherwise disguised it suggests it's someone known to her," said Jones.

Witts agreed and said, "My money is on the ex. He was obviously left disgruntled when she threw him out and he hasn't seen his daughter since then. I can't really believe that line she gave that he doesn't want to know. She's his daughter for heavens sake."

"I know," said Jones. "Another thing that strikes me as odd was why phone in the middle of the night like that. They could have phoned late before bedtime or first thing in the morning."

"I hadn't thought of that but yeah, that's weird as well."

"We need to take a closer look at Mary I think. Try and get some of these questions answered."

"You don't think she's involved do you? She seemed genuinely distraught as you'd expect her to be."

Jones nodded, "But we can't rule her out completely. I don't know what motive she would have for it but while we have question marks over some of what she said we can't make any assumptions."

"I know what you mean."

At this point they drew up at the office where Jez worked. That being the only contact details Mary had for him other than a phone number. The police wanted to take him by surprise in the hope of getting more out of him so hadn't phoned first. They entered the building and approached reception. The receptionist looked up with a friendly smile.

"We're looking for Jez Miller," said PC Jones.

"Jez? He doesn't work here."

"Oh? We were given this address for him."

"I'll call Matthew White down for you. He might be able to help. He's the manager."

WPC Witts raised her eyebrows at PC Jones. In her mind this was all very strange. "It seems odd that Mary didn't know this."

"I'm not sure, as they were estranged and there was a lot of acrimony between them."

"You could be right," said WPC Witts remaining unconvinced.

"Let's wait and see what we can find out first. We don't want to jump to conclusions."

At that moment a tall man entered reception with a smile he held out his hand to the two officers and introduced himself.

"Mr White nice to meet you. We are trying to get hold of Jez Miller," said Jones, taking the lead.

"Let's go through to my office then we can chat in comfort."

The two officers followed Matthew through what seemed like a maze of corridors eventually leading to an office. Matthew opened the door and stood aside saying, "Come in here. We won't be disturbed."

"We're WPC Witts and PC Jones," said Jones taking the lead.

"Nice to meet you. Now what can I do for you?"

"We are looking for a Jez Miller?"

"What's he done?" asked Matthew.

"We don't know that he's done anything yet. We need to speak to him on a matter of his daughter going missing."

"Oh no. Poor Mary, she must be distraught.

"You know her then?"

"Of course. She often accompanied Jez to office parties at Christmas. They always seemed the perfect couple. It's sad that they split up."

"So Jez did work here then?"

"Of course."

"Could you tell us why he left."

"I had to dismiss him. I gave him loads of chances but in the end I had no choice. I was sorry that I had to let him go he had always been a good worker. The best in my opinion. I had him pegged to be my replacement when I retired."

"You obviously think a lot of him."

Matthew nodded.

WPC Witts was taking notes which she and her colleague would go through later. She was leaving Jones to do the questioning.

"What happened?"

"It all started a few months before Jez and Mary split up. We had a new member of staff."

"Let me guess – female?"

Matthew nodded, saying, "You're getting the picture."

"It's not difficult to put two and two together and make four. They had an affair?"

Again Matthew nodded. "Sadly that's what happened. At first I didn't think anything of them always huddled with their heads together. I thought it was about work. Then they started leaving together early and going for a drink."

"Was this unusual for Jez?"

"Yes, most definitely. He always wanted to go home to Mary. We would invite him to have a drink at the end of the week with us but he always declined."

"What happened next?"

"I warned him to stay away from Miranda, that's her name."

"Does she still work here?" asked Witts, speaking for the first time.

Matthew shook his head. "She left last week. She was trouble."

"In what way?"

"She started seeing Clive who also works here. I couldn't have her splitting up another marriage. It always seemed to be the married ones she went for. She never gave a second glance to those who were single."

"Going back to Jez what happened to make him lose his job?"

Matthew sighed, "He started coming in later and later. He was no longer looking smart as he used to. He didn't look as if he'd shaved for weeks. His clothes were unkempt and he was starting to smell. He obviously wasn't looking after himself properly. I think he was also drinking too much although I had no proof of that."

"What about the quality of work?"

"That went down the pan as well. He always seemed to be staring off into space as if he wasn't hear at all. Other staff were complaining that he wasn't doing his share. He was losing us clients as he wasn't turning up to meetings and if he did they would complain about his appearance. It was starting to give us a bad reputation which I couldn't afford to let continue. I felt sorry for Jez but there was nothing I could do I had to protect the company."

"Is he working now?"

"I don't know. No one has asked me for a reference so I assume not."

"Can you give me an address for him?"

"I can, if he's still there. I think he's living with his current girlfriend."

"Name?"

"Sorry I don't know. Something like Anne, Anna, Anne-Marie."

"Ok thank you, you've been very helpful. We'll be off now we don't want to take up your precious time."

………

"That was interesting," commented WPC Witts.

"Certainly was. Very illuminating."

"What's our next move?"

"I still think the first thing is to get hold of Jez."

"You want us to go to the address Matthew gave us?"

PC Jones nodded.

Witts started the car and they drove following the sat nav to the address given.

"Well this is a far cry from where Mary lives. He has certainly hit rock bottom," said PC Jones when they drew up at the address.

The house was an end terrace. The white window frames were a horrible grey colour, definitely needing a lick of paint. The net curtains in the downstairs window also looked the worst for wear. Torn in places and also with a greyish tinge to them. The garden was looking overgrown and looked in need of urgent attention, there were plenty of weeds growing amongst the grass.

They got out of the car, not knowing what to expect when they got inside.

They rang the doorbell and waited. There was no sign or sound of movement inside. No twitching of curtains, nothing.

The officers looked at each other and rang again, this time Witts kept her finger on the bell. Still nothing.

"We're wasting our time, let's go. We'll come back later if we fail to track Mr Miller down," said Jones.

"Wait a minute," said WPC Witts as Jones was about to drive off. "I thought I saw a curtain twitch upstairs."

They stayed where they were for a moment watching for any further movement. There was nothing.

"I think we should try once more," said Witts.

Jones nodded and they went back to the house. Witts rang the bell while Jones stood back a bit looking up for any sign of movement.

"You're right I'm sure I saw a curtain twitch but no one appeared in the window. They kept themselves well hidden if there was anyone there."

Witts bent down to shout through the letter box. "Come on open up. We know there's someone there. We need to ask some questions and we're trying to trace down Jez Miller on a matter of urgency. It really is in your best interests to let us in."

Jones continued to look up and saw a window open and a woman's head poked out. "Jez isn't here. Why do you want him."

"Let us in we would prefer it if we didn't have to shout up to you for the whole neighbourhood to hear."

The lady gave a brief nod and closed the window. A few minutes later the door was opened. "I suppose you'd better come in if you insist."

The two officers stepped into the house. Witts wrinkled her nose at the smell which hit them the minute they stepped inside The interior looked as bad as the outside. There was just one room with an open plan kitchen attached. The sink was piled up with dirty dishes. The wallpaper was torn and hanging off.

"Take a seat," said the woman. "Cup of tea?"

The two officers quickly shook their heads. Who knew what they would catch if they were to drink out of dirty mugs.

"You said you're looking for Jez?"

Jones nodded whilst Witts took out her notepad.

"As I told you through the window he's not here."

"When will he be back?"

The woman shrugged, "Dunno."

"Are you expecting him back?"

Again the woman shrugged.

"Why don't you tell us your name?"

"Anne-Marie."

"How long has Jez been living here with you?"

"About three months."

"Where did you meet?"

"The pub on the corner of Kitchener Street."

"Does Jez work?"

"Dunno."

The officers looked at each other. This was like pulling teeth, hard work getting any information out of her. She wasn't exactly forthcoming.

"What does he get up to if he goes out all day."

"Who said he's out all day. I only said he's out at the moment."

"Well then, do you know when he'll be back."

Anne-Marie shrugged.

"Are you aware he had a phone call from his ex first thing this morning?"

"Of course. The phone rang loud enough."

"Do you know what it was about?"

"Something to do with his daughter but I don't know what?"

"Were you aware she's missing?"

Anne-Marie shrugged. "I didn't say I knew that."

"I know. I just asked the question. But you appear to know something so you might as well tell us everything."

Anne-Marie sighed, "Ok yes. I knew she had gone missing. Jez told her where to go though. He didn't want to know."

"Have you ever met Bethany?"

"Is that her name? No I haven't met her. I don't know anything about her and I don't want to. I made it very clear when Jez moved in here that he wasn't to have her here. I don't do children thank you very much."

The officers looked at each other. She really was a nasty piece of work. Who would want to keep someone from seeing their own daughter, or even preventing him talking to her.

"Can you tell us what time he'll be back, so we can speak to him?"

"Nope. Why should I? I'm not his keeper. He comes and goes as he pleases."

"Ok we'll leave you for now. If we need to we'll be back."

"Phew," said Witts as they got in the car. "I'm glad to get out of there. The place was terrible inside as well as out. She wasn't much better either. A far cry from Mary and her house."

"I know. Police work can bring us into contact with all sorts of people. That's one of the things I like about the job. It's varied. We meet all sorts within a shift sometimes."

"What did you make of Anne-Marie?"

"I don't know. I'm not entirely sure she was telling the truth."

"In what way?"

"I'm not sure. I can't put my finger on it."

"Do you think Jez was there?"

"I'm not saying that. I just don't know. It's a possibility though. She wasn't exactly going out of her way to help us even though she knew it was a missing child investigation."

"I know. You'd think she would be going out of her way to help."

"Oh well, let's move away from here. I'm quite sure she's still watching us to see if we have gone or not."

They drove away in silence, both lost in their own thoughts.

They didn't go far before Jones stopped the car again.

"Why have we stopped?"

"I just wanted to move around the corner and then I intended to phone Jez on the number Mary gave us. I didn't want to do this but it's important we track him down urgently. This could mean the difference between Mary getting her child back or not."

Witts nodded in understanding.

The phone rang and rang but no response. It went to voice mail. "Hello this is PC Jones. We need to speak to you about your daughter. It is a matter of some urgency so please contact me as soon as you get this message. I stress again the importance of speaking to you."

"Do you think he is deliberately avoiding us?" asked Witts.

Jones nodded. "From what we know so far, and admittedly that isn't much, I think it's possible."

The phone made a noise to indicate a message had been sent. Jones looked at it. "It's Jez," he said. "He doesn't want to speak to us. Says he has nothing to say about Bethany and insists it's nothing to do with him."

WPC Witts shook her head in disgust. "He sounds a right nasty piece of work. He doesn't even care about his own daughter."

"I'm not surprised actually. I did expect to get the brush off considering everything we've heard from Mary and Matthew. I think Anne-Marie knew more than she was letting on. I'm certain Jez was in the house."

"Should we go back there."

"Not at the moment. I don't think it would achieve anything."

"What's our next move?"

"You're to go back to Mary and see what else you can find out, maybe quiz her about the relationship between Jez and Bethany prior to the breakup. I'll drop you off before going back to the station."

Witts nodded in agreement. It made perfect sense to find out more about Jez and Bethany. At the moment Jez was at the top of her list of suspects. Admittedly there weren't any other suspects on it.

Chapter Three

Mary opened the door and eagerly looked passed Witts expecting to see her precious daughter returned to her. The smile disappeared as she realised Bethany wasn't there.

"Can I come in please?"

Mary moved aside, blushing as she said, "Yes, yes of course. I was just expecting Beth to be with you."

"Sorry we have no further news on that front. We have spent a lot of time since leaving you trying to trace Jez. We don't know where he is or how to contact him."

"Do you want a cup of tea or coffee?" asked Liz who was still with her friend, not liking to leave her in the state she had got herself in.

"Tea please, that would be lovely," answered the officer with a smile at Liz.

"But didn't you find him at work?" asked Mary.

Witts shook her head. "He doesn't work there anymore. We had quite a long conversation with Matthew about the situation."

"But why did Jez leave? I don't understand."

"He was sacked. He wasn't looking after himself after the breakup and also wasn't getting on with the work. He seemed more interested in flirting than doing the job. He was becoming a liability."

"We found out where he was supposed to be living but the woman that answered just said he wasn't in. She was being evasive to be quite honest."

"So he's with someone at the moment?"

The officer nodded, watching Mary carefully for a reaction.

Liz chose that moment to bring a tray of tea through from the kitchen. She passed the cups of tea around and offered sugar for those that wanted it. Taking a seat next to Mary she took hold of her hand and squeezed it hard, in a gesture of support. Mary looked at her gratefully. She had known Liz along time, and knew her to be very sensitive, always ready with a listening ear. Liz had been there right by her side when the break up had occurred. Liz had never taken to Jez. She had always felt Mary could do so much better.

There was silence for a few minutes as they all sipped their tea. It was Witts that broke it by saying, "We did try phoning after all attempts to find him came to nothing. PC Jones left a message for him and Jez responded almost immediately. He didn't want to know anything and basically refused to speak to us."

Mary looked distraught. "How will I ever get her back if Jez won't help. Is it possible he could be the one who took her."

"We don't know anything yet," said Witts carefully.

"Haven't you got any idea at all who is behind this."

"I'm very sorry. I know you want answers but anything we were to say at the moment would be pure speculation. We haven't got evidence either way."

Mary put her cup down hard on the table. So much so that it slopped over the side.

"Can you tell me more about Jez's relationship with Bethany right from a baby please. It might give us a way forward on this."

Mary nodded and stayed quiet for a time, lost in thought. Eventually she spoke.

"If I'm honest he has never shown any interest in her. Right from a newborn I had to do everything. He wouldn't cuddle her, change a nappy, get up to her in the night. Nothing. I dismissed it at the time thinking he just wasn't confident around babies but the situation didn't change as Beth got older. If anything it got worse. He wanted Beth kept out of the way. He didn't want noise or to be disturbed by children, At least that's what he said. If we went away he refused to let us go with Beth so we never went anywhere. I was never happy to leave her. He never wanted a child in the first place. When we first found out I was pregnant he ranted and raved and said no child was to be born. He wanted me to have an abortion, to which I refused."

Witts sighed and felt sadness at the story. It tugged at her heartstrings. She would never understand how some people could willingly abandon a poor innocent little baby. It seemed this was the case here.

"He never played games with her. He ignored her birthday and Christmas. We would just go to Liz over Christmas and leave Jez here on his own. As she got older he would insist she play in her room so he didn't have to see her. It was a reminder that he was a father and he didn't want that. Couldn't cope with it at all."

Witts leaned forward and patted Mary's hand. She really felt for her. From all she was hearing she thought it highly unlikely that Jez would kidnap his own daughter, there was no bond there at all. At first it had seemed as if it was a straight forward abduction by a father who had been cut off from his daughter's life and wanted more of her but evidence showed to the contrary.

"Is it possible he could have changed now he doesn't have any contact?"

"Changed? Jez? Unlikely!"

"Liz, what do you think about it?"

"She should never have married Jez. I said so at the time but she was so in love she was blind to what he's like. He was always flirting with other women before they were married and I didn't think that likely to change. Mary was always sticking up for him."

Mary nodded in agreement.

Witts asked, "How long have you two been friends?"

"Since school," said Mary.

"Where did you meet Jez?"

"It was Liz and her boyfriend. They were having a party and Jez was there. He was a close friend of Liz's boyfriend at the time. It was love at first sight on my part."

"When did you first become aware he was cheating on you?"

"The first time was eighteen months ago. I saw them together when I was waiting to meet Jez from work. He swore it was nothing. The floozy came on to him. I believed him until the next time it was another woman. I decided they couldn't all be throwing themselves at him. He tried talking his way out of it but I knew he was lying because I started following him to see for myself. I threw him out. He didn't try and talk his way out when he realised I had evidence. He blamed it on Beth. I lost it at that point. How could he say it was a small child that made him have an affair? He started on about he never wanted children and couldn't stand being around them."

Witts was busy scribbling down all this in case it was useful. It was background information if nothing else. It gave her an idea on how the people involved ticked. There was still a part of her that thought it possible that Jez had taken his daughter. He could have just been bluffing when talking to Mary. Spinning her a line. Even if he didn't want his daughter he could have taken her as a way of getting at Mary for throwing him out. Maybe there was some other more sinister motive for taking Beth.

It was all documented along with her own thoughts on the subject, to remind herself when she next got together with her colleague. There would be a debrief at some point either later or the next day.

………

"Well, how did you get on?" asked Jones within minutes of getting in the car after picking Witts up.

"It was interesting. I've got so much for you. I don't know how useful it is but it's a lot of background detail on how they functioned as a family."

Witts went on to tell him everything she had written down.

"You certainly have got a lot there. Well done. We'll tell the others back at the station and see if we can decide where to go from here."

"Did you get hold of Jez at all?"

Jones shook his head. "He never returned by call or text. It doesn't really surprise me, we know he's avoiding us. I want us to make a detour on the way back to the station. Maybe we'll catch him this time."

…….

"Why are you stopping around here?"

"I don't want them to see the car. They might drop their guard and open up for us."

"They'll see our uniforms," pointed out Witts.

"True but the car is more distinctive."

Jones put his finger on the bell and left if there. "This might get them answering the door. They'll do anything to stop the noise."

"Ok, ok," called a male voice as he approached the door.

Witts and Jones looked at each other with a look of victory. They'd tracked him down at last.

"Hello officers. How can I help?" asked the polite voice on opening the door.

"Jez Miller?" enquired Jones.

"Sorry no I'm Simon, you've got the wrong address."

Witts and Jones looked at each other with a look of confusion. "We were given the address only today. Do you know Jez?"

"Sorry I can't help you. Never heard of him."

"Anne-Marie seemed to know him this morning."

"Darling, it's the police at the door. Looking for a Jez."

Anne-Marie approached the door. She glowered at the officers and said, "I told you this morning he isn't here. Simon is my partner. Now can you go and leave us in peace. We know nothing."

The door was slammed shut abruptly before anything further could be said. The officers looked at each other. It seemed they had drawn a blank. He wasn't responding to his calls. He was no longer at work and seemed not to live at the last known address. An address which seemed to be false.

Where was Jez? Was he hiding out somewhere with Bethany?

"Where do we go from here? This is all very strange."

Jones nodded. "This makes me more suspicious of Jez. He clearly doesn't want to be found which in my book suggests he's guilty of something."

"I agree totally," said Witts. "My instincts were telling me that when I was speaking to Mary and Liz. Another thing that puzzles me was how did the kidnapper get in. Mary didn't let anyone in and there was no sign of a break in."

"You've got a good point there. It would have to be someone with a key."

"I'll find out who has keys to the house shall I?"

"Good thinking. What's your feeling about Mary?"

"I'm not sure. She seems completely distraught at the loss of her daughter."

"What about that phone call?"

"That's weird. Do you think it actually took place?"

Jones shrugged. "I'm just trying to look at every eventuality at the moment."

"I'll try and get more details about that. We don't even have a time it took place do we?" said Witts looking back through her notes. "No there's nothing here."

"There's quite a bit we still don't know that needs investigating. We haven't drawn complete blank yet."
"Could it still be someone we don't know and isn't known to Mary?"

"Unlikely. Most cases like this turn out to be family involvement and I'm sure this isn't any different especially as there's no break in and the child was taken from her bed. My thinking is it was someone she knew otherwise surely she would have screamed for Mary."

"True but she may have been told not to make a sound or she would never see her mother again. She's only a very young child she would have been terrified."

All talking had to stop as they arrived at the police station. They were ready for a debrief. Wondering how the rest of the team had got on with searching for Bethany. The fact that they hadn't heard anything wasn't hopeful. Time was crucial if they had any hope of finding her alive.

Chapter Four

Witts rang the doorbell the next morning. Mary was slow to answer. When she did Witts thought how terrible she looked. There were shadows under her reddened eyes and her general tousled appearance. She didn't look as if she'd gone to bed which was confirmed when Witts asked her.

"How could I? I needed to be awake in case Bethany came home."

Witts sighed. On the whole she enjoyed being a family liaison officer but it was times like today when it seemed unbearable. Seeing the pain in the parents of a missing child. The hope that their loved one would come home any minute. In Witts experience it very rarely ended happily. It always made Witts feel guilty when she had to ask difficult questions to see if it could be the parents who had taken the child. How could she believe Mary was guilty of anything when she saw how distraught she was. At the same time there were questions that must be asked and answered to rule Mary out of the equation.

"You haven't found her then?" asked Mary, with a note of despair in her voice, that Witts caught straight away.

Witts shook her head. "Shall I make us a nice cup of tea? I don't suppose you've had breakfast have you?"

"I haven't eaten since. I can't. I'll be sick if I do."

"You must try or you'll be ill, then what will Bethany do when she comes home?"

"You think she will then?" asked Mary latching on to a glimmer of hope Witts seemed to be offering.

"We're doing everything we can to find her. By the way call me Carol. It sometimes helps to be able to call your officer by name."

Mary nodded but made no reply. Carol went through to make a cup of tea for them both and a slice of toast for Mary.

Both ready she took them back through to the living room where Mary was sat silently weeping. Mary pushed the plate of toast away, she really didn't feel able to eat anything. She was sure she would bring it back up again.

Carol sipped her tea whilst keeping a close eye on Mary who made no attempt to eat or drink anything.

"You must have something you'll be ill otherwise."

Mary shrugged, "What does it matter? I'm nothing without Beth. She was my life especially when my marriage fell apart."

"Have you any more thoughts as to the whereabouts Jez might be?"

"Haven't you found him yet?"

"No. We went back to the house which was the last known address for him but there was another man living there who said he didn't know anyone called Jez."

"What about the phone?"

"Nothing. He's not answering or sending a text. It's as if he never existed."

There was silence for a while. Mary picked up the cup and sipped the sweet tea. Carol had made sure to put plenty of sugar in it to help since Mary wasn't eating.

"What was the name of the man you spoke to?" asked Mary suddenly.

"Simon. Why, do you know him?"

"Simon, that's Jez's middle name."

"Right I must ring the station and let them know. PC Jones might be able to go round there again."

Carol jumped up with her phone and went into the hallway to make the call.

"Adam? We might have something here. Mary just said that Jez's middle name is Simon."

"What? So we were actually talking to Jez. That's interesting. I wonder why he wanted to avoid talking to us. I'm on my way to pick you up and we'll go straight round there."

Carol went back to Mary after disconnecting the call and told her what was going to happen.

Mary nodded but stayed silent.

Carol tried to think of the best way to approach the subject of keys.

"Keys? What has that got to do with anything?"

"Well the kidnapper seems to have got in without breaking in. They can't have done that without a key unless you let them in."

"Which I definitely didn't. I still don't understand how they could have got upstairs without waking me. I'm a light sleeper and the third step squeaks every time it's stood on."

"Hmm," said Carol. "Anyway back to the subject of keys."

"Jez had one of course but he gave it back. I remember clearly as he threw it at me and it hit my face."

"Anyone else?"

Mary thought for a few minutes before shaking her head, "There's no one else."

"What about Liz? She's a close friend."

Mary shook her head. "Anyway she wouldn't take Beth. Why would she when she has her own son who's the same age as Beth."

"Ok, could Jez have cut a key when he still had it?"

"Why would he do that? That means he knew I was going to throw him out and that he would do something like this."

It was at that moment that Jones pulled up in an unmarked car. Carol said goodbye to Mary and went out.

"Any more info?" asked Jones as she got in the car.

"Give me a chance to get in then."

"Sorry I was just desperate for as much information as possible if we are to confront Jez."

"He is the only one with a key but he gave that back when Mary threw him out. I also discovered that the kidnapper must have known the house because the third stair squeaks which would have woken Mary up but it didn't. Whoever it was avoided that stair."

"Interesting, so it must be someone close to home then. This seems to strengthen the case against Jez."

Carol nodded. "Mary, by the way, is absolutely distraught, not eating or drinking. Not even dressed."

"What do you think about her?"

"I'm still not sure. The case of the phone call still haunts me. I must ask about that when we've finished with Jez."

Jones nodded. He liked Carol. She was excellent at her job and managed to get information from families that no one else could. She had good instincts and would go far in her career he was certain of that.

They quickly pulled up around the corner again and got out of the car.

"Hopefully we'll catch them as we are so early. They won't expect us this early. It all looks shut up and quiet."

Jones rang the doorbell keeping his finger on it as he did yesterday. They waited but nothing.

"If you're looking for Anne-Marie, you'll have a long wait. They packed the car with suitcases and went last night," called a voice from over the hedge, separating the two houses.

"Thank you. And you are?"

"Mrs Murray."

"Was she alone?"

Mrs Murray shook her head. "That boyfriend of hers went with her. He seemed in an awful hurry."

The two officers looked at each other. "Was there a child?" asked Carol.

"No, they haven't got children."

"Do you know how long they have been together."

"About three months. I didn't like him from the start. There was something about him that I couldn't stand and I warned Anne-Marie about him. She always picks the wronguns."

"In what way didn't you like him?"

"That shifty look in his eye and he used to flirt with every young woman he came across. I did warn her but she could see no wrong."

"Have you any idea where they might have gone. Any family they could have gone to."

Mrs Murray shrugged, "Anne-Marie never mentioned anyone and no one ever visited. I used to think how sad it was that she so young had no one."

"Well thank you, ma'am you've been a big help," said Adam Jones. He could see they would be stood there all day if he didn't finish the conversation.

Mrs Murray gave a big smile. She was already thinking of the tale she'd have to tell him in doors when she went back in. She'd be dining out on this one for ages. The only thing was she didn't have any clue as to why the police wanted the couple. She would have to find out somehow, or her imagination would fill in the gaps. She wasn't known as the neighbourhood busy body for nothing. She always said if any one asked that it was for him. He never went out, except to hospital appointments so relied on her gossip. It gave him something to live for. She realised she was getting muddled again. As with it when it came to gossip as she was, she kept forgetting her husband was no longer there. He had died the previous year.

"Now what?" asked Carol getting back in the car.

"I don't know. It never occurred to me that they would go AWOL."

"That's because we didn't know that Simon was in fact Jez! I can't believe how they pulled the wool over our eyes like that."

"I would put a message out to keep a lookout for them but we don't know car details. He could easily have changed his car since being with Mary so I don't think she'll be able to help."

"Why don't we go back and ask the neighbour. She was quite happy to be of help and if I'm right she doesn't miss anything."

"Good thinking."

They walked slowly back to Mrs Murray. She must have been watching out the window as she was opening the door before they rang the bell.

"Sorry to trouble you again."

"That's no problem. I'm always happy to help you people. You do a good job at keeping us safe."

"We do our best," said Adam. "You don't happen to know the details of the car do you. As much as you can."

"Come in. I happen to have it written in my little book."

Carol raised her eyebrows at Adam as they went in. They'd definitely struck gold with Mrs Murray. If only everyone were like her, it would make their job much easier.

"Take a seat for a minute," said Mrs Murray, picking up a thick note pad and flicking through the pages.

Carol glanced around the room which seemed devoid of all photos. In fact they room was surprisingly bare except for three overstuffed chairs which looked most uncomfortable.

"Here we are," said Mrs Murray after a few minutes. "Silver. GO2 9LL."

"Great. Thank you so much for your help. You're a star," said Adam.

Mrs Murray's face lit up at the compliment. It was nice to feel useful for once. Truth be told she was a lonely lady in her sixties, with no family around her. She hadn't been blessed with children and her much loved husband had died the previous year. It was before his death she started taking an interest in the neighbours and what they were doing. He was housebound and frustrated. He missed having a chat with people in the street and in the shops. After his death she kept it up as it gave her something to do and occasionally she had a really juicy titbit. She didn't like the way everyone kept themselves to themselves these days. Not like it used to be at all when there was a real sense of community and everyone helped each other. She wasn't popular and found people did their best to avoid her, even turning and going in the opposite direction if they saw her.

....

Carol put the message out for officers to look out for the car and to stop them and take them to the station if found.

Adam drove off. He always did the driving, having an old fashioned view that women weren't safe. It annoyed Carol but she kept it to herself. It gave her more time to put some thought into the case they were working on.

"Drop me off at Mary's will you. I'll update her and see what else I can get from her."

Adam didn't speak just nodded, wanting to concentrate on this stretch of road which had some nasty junctions and roundabouts to negotiate. Arriving safely at Mary's, Carol got out the car and waved goodbye to Adam.

In many ways Carol enjoyed working on her own with a family rather than always with another officer. It meant she could use her brain and reason things out for herself. She was often able to solve the case from the information given. She found it hard though if she were close to a family and then discovered they were the perpetrators after all. On the opposite side it could be more difficult as she has no one to talk her thoughts through with that can bring clarity to a situation.

Carol found Mary still not dressed or showered. She looked as if she hadn't moved from the sofa where Carol had last left her. The evidence was plain to see with a soggy pile of tissues. Carol tried not to feel too sympathetic as she couldn't get passed how it could have happened without Mary knowing anything.

"Hello Mary, why don't you have a shower and get dressed while I make us a nice cup of tea."

"I can't in case Beth comes home."

"It's all right I'm here to answer the door." What Carol didn't add was that it was unlikely that Beth would just turn up without the police knowledge. If it were to happen it would have done so by now.

"Do you have a basement or anything?" asked Carol suddenly. She had an idea occur to her and wanted to check it out while she was still thinking about it.

"No basement but we do have a loft."

"Ok. How do we access it?"

"Jez always used to get a ladder and go up there. I've never done it. It seems unsafe to me and I can't stop thinking of what might be up there. Spiders and other awful creatures probably. UGH! Can't stand them. I always have had a severe phobia."

"Where is a ladder so I can go up and check it out?" asked Carol.

"It's in the garage."

Carol went out to fetch it at the same time wondering if there was a reason for Mary's reluctance to get up there. She didn't like what she was thinking but at this point it was essential to check everywhere even the unlikely places.

Carol took her time going up the ladder. She was a bit nervous herself but didn't want Mary to see it as she didn't want to hear any more excuses as to why they shouldn't do anything.

When up there and in the loft Carol took in a at a glance that there was a lot of stuff up there. She could only believe that Jez had been storing things without Mary's knowledge. That in itself seemed like suspicious activity to her. She would have to pass this on. Certainly at a glance it was so packed that there was no space to hide a child.

Whilst up there she took a quick look at some of the boxes to see if there were any note to suggest what was in them. She noticed one saying photo albums and had a quick glance in it. Inside she found albums with photos of young children. This raised a red flag in her mind. This whole loft was going to have to be searched thoroughly, but for the meantime she took the album to take down and see if Mary recognised any of the children in the photos.

"What's this?" asked Mary when Carol handed her the photo album.

"Do you recognise this at all?"

Mary looked at it and shook her head, certain she had never seen it before.

"You've never seen Jez with this?"

"No, definitely not. He's not keen on children which is why he's never shown interest in Beth."

"Look through it please and then tell me if you recognise anything in these photos."

Mary started flicking through the album, her face paling as she gave it a cursory glance.

"Here sit down," said Carol, as Mary started swaying, ashen faced.

"What is this? I've never seen it before and these children, who are they?"

"And you're sure you've never been up there."

"No I told you. Why?"

"I'm afraid I will have to take this away with me and if I'm right we will have to search the loft thoroughly to see what's up there."

Mary nodded vaguely, not fully taking in what she was seeing and hearing. Life had turned into a complete nightmare.

Carol went outside to make a quick call then went back in to speak to Mary. "Yes, it's been confirmed by my Sergeant. We need to see what else is up there. A team will be here later today as soon as it can be set up."

Mary put her head in her hands and sighed. What on earth was this all about?

Carol was also wondering. The investigation in what had seemed a clear cut case of child abduction had taken an unexpected turn and now it looked like a paedophile may have been involved. In her mind Jez had to be the prime suspect as it was all at his house. Were there others involved? Why did he leave them with Mary instead of taking them with him? Too many questions and as yet no answers. What was becoming obvious was that they needed to speak to Jez as soon as they could possibly find him. Now at least they could understand why he would run away. He had something much bigger to hide.

Chapter Five

"Ok everyone listen up,"

There was an immediate silence around the room. Officers turned and looked at Sergeant Macintosh.

"As you all know the investigation into the disappearance of little Bethany Miller has taken an unexpected turn and images have been found of young girls about Bethany's age in a photo album. Now we need to search the whole loft and see what else we can find. Carol has done a good job in discovering a photo album and she says there are loads of other boxes filling the loft. Today we have to empty the loft and then systematically go through each box and see what they contain. Carol will keep Mrs Miller away from the house while we do this. We don't want to upset her more than we have to."

. . . .

"Are you ready Mary?" asked Carol, who was in a hurry so the search team could get on with the job as quickly as possible. Time was of the essence here.

"Yes," said Mary. She had just put a coat and shoes on. She hadn't bothered to change or put a brush through her long hair.

"How about combing your hair," said Carol.

Mary shook her head. "I can't be bothered. It's not worth it without my Beth."

"You think she would want to come home to a mum who has given up and doesn't care what she looks like. She might say she doesn't even know you looking like that."

Reluctantly Mary went back up to the bathroom and gave her hair a quick brush. She didn't even look in the mirror as she did it.

Carol said nothing when Mary went back downstairs where she was waiting. At least an effort of sorts had been made.

"I thought we could go and sit in the park as it's a nice day. We could get a cup of tea at the café there or an ice cream."

Mary shrugged. She didn't care what they did anymore. Her life had been wrapped around her daughter and now she had no one which gave her an empty feeling. Something was missing in her life and she didn't have the will to carry on. She couldn't think about the possibility that she might never see Beth again.

Carol tried to make small talk on the way to the park but got no response from Mary. She gave up and they continued in silence. They chose to sit on the bench nearest to the car park. Mary couldn't be bothered to do anything else.

Suddenly a dog went running up to Mary and sniffed at her, putting her front feet up on to the bench. Mary couldn't help herself and reached down to stroke the dog.

"Sorry to bother you," said a woman hurrying up to them. "Strike come down leave the two ladies alone."

"It's ok," whispered Mary.

Strike ignored the woman and stayed there making squeaking noises. Mary felt emotion well up inside and the tears started to fall. Unable to help herself she buried her head in Strike's fur and cried.

"I'm so sorry," said the woman. "I didn't mean to upset you."

"You haven't," said Carol. "She's just having a difficult time right now."

"Oh I'm sorry to hear that. I'm Barbara by the way."

"Nice to meet you," said Carol.

Mary ignored the conversation between the other two women and continued to cry into Strike.

"I bet he sensed your friend was struggling. He's a very sensitive dog and likes to give comfort."

"He's certainly doing that," said Carol.

Mary's tears stopped and she lifted her head. Her face was a mess with reddened, swollen eyes and tear stained cheeks.

"Come on Strike," said Barbara. Strike seeing that his job was done got down and followed Barbara away from the women.

"Did that help?" asked Carol.

"You know I think it may have. There was something so comforting and innocent about Strike."

"Well, they do say how intuitive dogs are. More so than cats who are more independent."

"I don't like cats," said Mary. "I would have loved to have a dog though, but Jez always said no. He hates all animals, or so he said."

"There is nothing to stop you getting one now you're not with him."

"True, I'll think about it. I'm sure Beth would love a dog. She's always clamouring for a pet. One of her friends at school has a rabbit. She always talks about it when she gets home from her friends house."

"What about her friends? Are you friendly with any of their mums."

"Yes sort of. We say hello in the playground and arrange for play dates."

"Why don't you arrange to meet up with some of them."

"It would feel awkward now Beth isn't with me. Neither of us would know what to say."

Carol nodded in understanding. "Can you give me some names and addresses so we can speak to them to see if they can shed any light on to the situation."

"I'm sure they won't be able to help."

"Possibly not, but we have to explore all eventualities."

Carol's phone rang at that moment so they fell silent while she answered. "Ok serge we're on our way."

"They've finished now," said Carol turning to Mary.

They stood up and started to make their slow way back.

Arriving back at the house they found the living room to look like a demolition site with torn up boxes everywhere.

"Sorry about the mess," said the Sergeant. "We will take all this with us and put it in the recycling. Your loft will seem empty up there now as we have taken everything."

"It doesn't matter to me," said Mary. "I never go up there. To me it seems unsafe." She looked around the room before adding, "I didn't even know we had this much stuff up there."

"We were shocked as well."

"Can you tell me what was there?"

"More photo albums and a couple of videos. They all contain the same sort of thing as the one Carol found. I'm afraid we may have stumbled across a paedophile ring."

Mary was stunned, although she supposed she shouldn't have been after seeing the album Carol had shown her.

"At some point I am afraid we may have to ask you to have a look at them to see if you recognise any of the children. They may be friends of Bethany's."

"I don't think I can do that," said Mary. "It's too horrible to even think about."

"I'm sorry. I know it is but we'll still need you. Don't worry we won't show you everything. If there is anything distressing in them we won't show you."

Mary nodded.

"Before we go Mary has agreed to give us the name of some of Bethany's friends and their parents."

"Brilliant good work Carol."

Mary went to the kitchen and picked up some note paper and a pen and began to write. It took a while as she had to stop and think several times. Eventually she finished and went back to the hall where Carol and Sergeant Macintosh were standing. She handed the note to Carol who thanked her.

"I'll have to go back to the station now and help look through all this evidence. I'll be back later today or tomorrow if I have any news. We have plenty to keep us busy and out of mischief anyway."

Mary smiled at that last sentence. She had a feeling that out of work Carol might have a strong sense of humour which Mary appreciated having a weird sense of humour herself. Not that there was any sign of it quite understandable under the circumstances. In fact Mary couldn't imagine ever laughing again.

Once on her own Mary sank down on to the sofa and leaned her head back. She was so tired and could just fall asleep but she tried by all means to keep her eyes open. She didn't want to and possibly miss Beth arriving back home. A part of her was also scared that if she let go and closed her eyes she would have nightmares.

She fell into a light doze to be woken by the phone.

"Hello," she said.

"Mary. You. Ignored. My. Instructions. Last. Time. And. Now. You. Done. Something. Very. Stupid. And. Called. The. Cops."

Mary gasped as she listened to the robotic voice again.

"Who are you?" she asked.

No response. There was silence and Mary wondered if that was the end of the call. She was about to put the phone down when the voice started again." Go. To. Liz. She'll. Tell. You. What. To. Do. Next. I. look. Forward. To. Our. Conversation. Again. Soon."

The phone was disconnected and Mary sat there looking at it. Why Liz she wondered. Had her best friend betrayed her? That didn't make sense. She was sure Liz wouldn't do anything to upset her and certainly wouldn't take Beth. Why would she when she had children of her own.

Mary immediately phoned Carol and told her about the call.

"Just a minute, I'll speak to the Serge and see what he advises."

There was silence on the line except for voices in the background.

"Yes, go round to see Liz but don't say anything much about the call. We don't want her to close up if she does know anything. I'll pick you up from there in about an hour."

Mary thanked her and put the phone down. For some reason she felt very anxious at going to see her friend. She didn't know why. Maybe it was to do with the possibility that Liz might know what was happening and be involved in some way.

....

Liz was quick to open the door to her friend. She started to smile until she saw the evidence of Mary's tears. "Beth still not back then," she said looking past Mary expecting the little girl to go running up to be picked up by her auntie Liz. Liz stood aside to let Mary in.

"Oh Liz it's so awful. I don't know what I'll do if she never comes back. I can't bear the thought of never seeing my little girl again."

"I'm sure she'll turn up soon."

"How can you be so sure?"

"I'm just trying to think positively. I want to encourage you not drag you down further."

Mary nodded, but remembering that voice she couldn't quite trust her friend. Was she saying this because she knew something? She wished Carol were with her. She would know straight away what to say to get any information Liz might have on the whereabouts of Beth, her darling daughter.

"I hope she's being well looked after wherever she is," said Mary. She was desperate to start a conversation about Beth's whereabouts to see if Liz did indeed know something.

"Hmm," said Liz. In her mind she was not as hopeful as Mary. She didn't want to upset her friend though, who needed something positive to cling on to. She was a realist and from what she'd seen on the telly especially the news, kidnapped children never ended happily. Bodies were found or sometimes there was a permanent state of limbo where the body was never found and the child never returned. She hoped that last would not be like that for Mary. A body they could cope with and she would be there for Mary to help her through it.

Mary was getting frustrated. Liz wasn't giving anything away. It was unlike Liz to be so silent. Did that mean she knew something and wasn't saying? Maybe she'd been warned to keep her mouth shut. Yes, that was it. She was being forced into something she didn't want to be involved in. Mary was quick to seize the thought, the alternative being unbearable as it would mean she would ultimately lose her friend.

"Anyway instead of standing here like idiots shall I put the kettle on for a cuppa?"

"Oh yes please. You know me I never say no."

Liz was pleased Mary was agreeing to a drink as she had lost weight over the short time Beth had been missing. She knew Mary wasn't eating. She didn't realise Mary was only agreeing to buy more time to find out anything Liz might know.

In her mind Mary was becoming convinced that she'd been sent on a wild goose chase. Liz didn't appear to know anything.

"Have you heard anything more from that police woman, what's her name?" asked Liz when she sat down with the teas.

"Carol. Yes and they searched my house. Carol took me out while it was done."

"Why on earth would they search your house. Surely they don't expect to find Beth hidden there. That's too ludicrous to even think about."

"No it isn't that. Carol went up into the loft and found loads of boxes….." Mary stopped, unsure as to whether she should tell Liz all this but no one had said it was confidential had they.

"Boxes! But you never went up there."

"I know. It must have been Jez. He was hiding…… hiding something that he didn't want discovered. He must have forgotten to take them when he moved out, or more likely didn't want them found by anyone. He knew I never went up there so knew they were safe there."

"What was in the boxes? You've got me intrigued now."

"I'm not sure if I should say," said Mary.

"You can't say this much and then keep quiet. That's not fair."

"Well ok, but don't tell anyone."

"Of course not. Do I ever spread what we've talked about?"

Mary looked ashamed of herself. It was true Liz never told anyone anything, even things that didn't matter she didn't pass on.

"You'll never believe it. I couldn't when Carol showed them to me. The boxes contained photo albums. The photos were all of different young girls."

"But Jez has never shown interest in Beth so why loads of girls?"

"That's what I thought but the police are taking it seriously. The other boxes are also full of photos of young children apparently. I haven't seen them yet. They do want me to look at some point after they've finished to see if I can identify any of the children."

Liz nodded, but said nothing. What was there to say? She couldn't pretend she wasn't shocked. She didn't want to say what she was thinking in case Mary was completely innocent as to what it might mean. Paedophilia was uppermost in her mind. Surely not? If this had been a drama on telly or a novel maybe but this was real life. Most ordinary people would never come near to a paedophile. It still seemed unbelievable that Jez might be one. Unless he was just hiding the photos for a friend. But then surely he would have to know what was in the albums. It was totally unbelievable that he didn't look or wasn't told what they contained. Yes which ever way one looked at it Jez had to be involved.

Mary sipped her tea, lost in her own thoughts. She was going to have to leave and admit to Carol that she'd failed in her mission to get the longed for information out of her friend.

The two women sat in an awkward silence, neither knowing what to say to the other. This was rare for them as usually they would talk nineteen to the dozen. It just goes to show how uncomfortable people are around someone else's tragedy.

"Well I suppose I should go. I can't stay here indefinitely," said Mary, finishing her tea.

Liz was relieved although she didn't want to show that. She felt awkward around Mary, not knowing what to say to comfort her friend. This tragedy so close to home was making Liz over protective of her own son.

As soon as Mary was out of sight of her friend, she stopped and took her phone from her bag and called Carol. Carol wasn't surprised. She hadn't been convinced by the phone call Mary had received.

"Look stay where you are. I'm coming to pick you up and bring you to the station. We need you to look through photos for us."

"Ok," said Mary, telling Carol where she was.

Chapter Six

"Get in," said Carol drawing alongside Mary.

"I don't think I can do this. Do I have to?"

Carol nodded. "It would be very helpful to us."

"But it might not have anything to do with Beth's disappearance."

"It might not, but we still have to investigate all lines of enquiry."

Mary nodded, feeling very apprehensive.

Carol left her to her thoughts, feeling it best not to say anything further. She knew for sure that team were of the opinion they had stumbled across a paedophile ring and were fairly certain that Beth had been taken by them. What they needed to do was identify the other girls and work out if they had gone missing as well. They hadn't found any photos of Beth in the collection but that didn't mean anything.

Arriving at the station Carol ushered her in. Officers turned to look at her, wanting to see this woman whose husband was allegedly a paedophile who may have taken his own daughter to satisfy his sick cravings. Mary reddened under their stares.

"Here we go," said Carol opening a door to the right. Inside was a small room containing a table and two rickety chairs. There was what looked like a mirror at one side. Although Mary didn't know it there were members of CID the other side watching and taking notes of Mary's interview.

It had been agreed that Carol was the best person to show Mary the photos as she had some sort of rapport with her.

"Ok Mary, I'm going to show you some photos and I want you to say if you recognise anyone. Take your time, there is no rush."

The first few of the pile went through quickly as Mary could see straight away that she didn't know anyone. Then came a photo that Mary assumed she would pass straight on like the others but she paused. At first she wasn't sure but the more she looked the more she became convinced that she recognised a child.

"What is it Mary do you recognise someone?"

"Possibly," said Mary in a small voice, just above a whisper.

"Ok, take your time," said Carol in a soothing voice, aimed at calming the worried woman.

Mary looked but the more she did she wasn't so sure after all. What if she made a mistake? It seemed too important to get wrong and cause distress needlessly to someone.

"I…I'm not so sure now," said Mary.

"It's ok. We can put it to one side and we'll come back to it later," said Carol not at all perturbed.

The next few passed quickly without incident until another one was shown to Mary. She gasped instantly. She couldn't believe what she was seeing. She looked away then looked back. No, she wasn't mistaken. It was Beth but a younger version.

"Who is it?" asked Carol, gently.

"B…B…It's Beth," said Mary, breaking down into wracking sobs.

Her daughter had been got at by a paedophile ring. How could she have not known? What made it worse was that Beth was completely naked. Oh God what had happened to her and what was she going through now? She couldn't bear it.

Carol was shocked. They hadn't expected Beth to be amongst the girls. They had thought that the girls were kidnapped by the ring and then used and abused, but this suggested otherwise. Did this mean that the others would disappear at some point if they hadn't already? This was looking like a race against time to prevent other young girls from being abused and for other families to be torn apart.

Carol went out and caught an officer walking by and asked for some water for Mary.

"Here sip this. It'll help."

Mary shook her head at first but then gave in. It quietened the sobbing but she was in shock.

"Are you able to carry on?" asked Carol.

Mary nodded. "Let's get it over with. I could never rest if I knew I still had to do this."

Carol understood and said, "We can stop at any time, you just have to say the word."

Silence reigned as Carol continued to show Mary photos and Mary shook her head, indicating she didn't know the girl in the photo.

"That's Maddy," said Mary. "She's in Beth's class at school. They were friends until recently when Maddy suddenly withdrew. Beth was hurt as she didn't know what she'd done."

Carol glanced at the mirror, sure that the detectives sitting on the other side would be thinking the same as her. Maddy may have withdrawn because of the abuse she may have suffered. The next step would be to talk to Maddy and see what she knew.

The photos kept coming but Mary didn't recognise anyone else.

"You've done really well," said Carol.

"But I only recognised two and one of them was my Beth."

"That's better than what we had before we started. We have at least got a line of enquiry now which we can follow."

"Really?"

"Yes. I'll take you home now and you can rest. I'll be in touch as soon as I can, but I think I'll be needed here."

Chapter Seven

"So what line are we taking?" asked Carol, when they reached Maddy's house.

"You are taking the lead once we get to talk to Maddy," said DC John Mayhew. "We'll start by asking her general questions about school and then move on to her friendship with Beth. We'll see where that takes us and go from there."

Carol nodded.

Maddy's mum opened the door a crack and peered through the gap. "Yes?" she asked.

"Police," said Carol showing her id badge.

"What do you want?"

"We need to ask Maddy some questions. Her name came up in relation to the disappearance of Beth Miller."

"I'm sure she doesn't know anything but come in anyway."

"Why do you say she doesn't know anything. From what we hear they were good friends."

"Until recently. Maddy seems to have had a falling out. They haven't spoken since then Maddy won't tell me what happened but she's been very upset. I don't what you upsetting her further."

"Don't worry, we'll be very gentle and you are allowed to sit in as she is so young. We don't think she's done anything wrong if that helps at all."

....

Maddy looked at the officers clearly intimidated. She moved closer to her mum, sucking her thumb making Carol feel guilty for having to ask questions of someone so young.

"Hello Maddy, my name's Carol. I'm helping to look for Beth. I hear she's a friend of yours."

Maddy shook her head.

"Your mummy said you fell out and you're not friends anymore."

Maddy nodded.

"Can you tell me what happened?"

"We were drawing," said Maddy, taking her thumb out of her mouth just long enough to speak.

"What about drawing? Were you drawing something nice."

Maddy nodded. "I was drawing mummy and daddy."

"That's sounds nice. I bet you're good at it as well."

Maddy continued speaking, "Mr Stubbs asked me to stay behind when everyone else went out to play."

"Ok," said Carol, alarm bells ringing in her head. "What did he want you for."

"He said he'd spoken to Beth as well."

Maddy became silent as the tears started to fall.

"It's all right Maddy. You've been a good girl telling us this much. Can you tell us anymore."

Maddy shook her head starting to look scared. Carol noticed this and knew she would have to tread extra carefully. They had obviously found something which she could guess at but they needed to hear it from Maddy.

"It's all right," said her mum. "Tell the lovely lady what you know. You're not in any trouble." Her voice shook as she spoke, frightened at what they might find out.

"He said not to tell or I'd never see you again."

The adults gasped unable to hide their horror. It was becoming very clear what they were dealing with. There were tears in her mum's eyes as the truth also dawned on her.

"You haven't done anything wrong. You'll see your mummy and daddy again. Nothing will happen to you or them," said Carol gently.

"Beth must have told that's why she's gone missing."

"Oh darling. You won't go missing we'll make sure of that," said her mum.

"He told me to take my clothes off. He helped me when I struggled with my buttons and shoe laces."

This was too much even for someone who should have become hardened to this. Carol's eyes filled with tears and she had to look away. This was a harrowing experience and it didn't get any easier the more she did it.

"Ok I think we'll stop for today," said John, speaking for the first time.

"Mrs Merriweather we may have to ask more questions but Maddy isn't up to telling us more. Just to warn you we may have to have her examined by our doctor to get any evidence."

Mrs Merriweather nodded but didn't say anything. She didn't know what to say. All she wanted to do was tell her husband and then for the three of them to move far away from the town. Somewhere they could protect Maddy where she would be no more at risk.

The teachers were supposed to teach and protect the children in their care not abuse them.

"You will get him won't you?" she asked.

"We'll do our best," said John.

. . . .

"You did a good job in there," said John when they were on their way back to the station.

"It doesn't feel like it right now."

"Well you did. We now have at least one name of those involved. With any luck he'll be happy to give us everything we need to know so we can close down this ring and reunite Beth with Mary."

"Do you think she's still alive?" asked Carol.

"I don't know," sighed John, "But we have to stay positive and hope she is."

"Are we even sure this is the work of paedophiles? After all I can't get passed the fact that there was no break in and Mary seems certain Jez is the only one with the key. I think there are things about that family we don't know about. Secrets hidden."

"You could be right. I wasn't thinking along those lines. I was thinking it was too much of a coincidence that we discover a paedophile ring at the same time a young child goes missing."

"I know but I don't believe it's that simple."

"Your instincts are usually good so I'll keep an open mind on the subject for now."

....

As soon as Adam saw Carol he knew which direction things were going. The distress on her face was enough to tell him.

"You don't look great."

"I don't feel it either," said Carol quietly.

"It's not good then. I was hoping for the best here and that we would have been mistaken."

"No such luck. It looks as if we were going in the right direction. The art teacher told her not to say anything or she wouldn't see her parents again."

Adam gasped. He couldn't believe what he was hearing. That was enough to traumatise anyone but a little girl of six it would have been terrifying. He shook his head unable to get away from the images coming into his mind.

"I know," said Carol. "It doesn't matter how much you hear it, it never gets any easier does it."

Adam shook his head unable to speak. The words wouldn't come. He was just imagining what was happening. What could be happening right now with a little girl.

"What happens now?" he asked eventually.

"We have to speak to Mr Stubbs. I must go back and update Mary. I want to also question her about the key situation. I can't get out of my mind that there is more to that."

"You don't think it's linked?"

Carol paused before answering. "No I don't think I do. I'm not sure Mary is telling us everything."

"Do you think she's involved in her daughter's disappearance?"

"I'm not sure but I think it's a possibility. CID are taking over now we've uncovered a potential paedophile ring but I'm still the family liaison officer so I can continue delving into that."

"I'm with you on that. Your instincts are usually spot on."

"I hope I'm wrong. I don't like to think of Mary being involved because in spite of my thoughts I like her."

"I know what you mean. I do as well. There is something about her. I think it's her apparent vulnerability." said Adam.

"I think you've got it spot on. I couldn't think what it was but you've put it into words. She seems so desperate about her daughter which surely can't be an act."

"I know. But remember we've seen it before. Parents pulling the wool over our eyes I mean."

"I know that."

"We rely on your intuition when it comes to the family. You spend more time with them, getting to know them."

They stopped outside Mary's house and Carol got out. "Let me know what happens with Mr Stubbs," said Carol before shutting the car door.

"Will do," said Adam.

……

Carol was sitting on the sofa with Mary sipping a cup of tea. Carol couldn't help thinking what a nice cup Mary made. It was perfect not too weak but not too strong either. They were in silence. Mary was waiting for Carol to take the lead. As the silence went on Mary became uncomfortable.

"What happened about the photos?" asked Mary eventually. Unable to bear the silence any longer.

"We went to see Maddy and had a chat with her."

"Yes."

"Did Bethany ever mention a Mr Stubbs?" asked Carol, seeing nothing for it but to come straight to the point.

Mary looked startled and said, "He's her art teacher. I've met him at parent teacher evenings. He seems a very caring person who takes an interest in the children. He thinks Beth might have a talent."

This rang alarm bells in Carol. She supposed it was an ordinary thing to say but knowing what she did it was worrying.

"Has Bethany ever talked about him?" asked Carol again.

"Not excessively. She isn't keen on art though and is reluctant to go to school when she knows she'll be having art."

"Has she always been like this?"

Mary thought for a while before saying, "Now I come to think of it I don't think so. It wasn't a particularly favourite subject but she didn't like or dislike it. Lately though, she has been protesting about it and trying to get out of going to school."

"Is that unusual for her?"

"Yes. She used to love school, in fact I think she still does, except for art that is."

"Maddy mentioned not liking art either although it seemed Mr Stubbs she disliked more than anything."

"Did she say why she stopped playing with Beth?" asked Mary curious to know what had happened with the two girls.

Carol didn't know what to say without giving everything away. She knew Mary deserved to know the truth but she wanted to wait until Mr Stubbs had been spoken to, not wanting to cause Mary further distress until she had to.

"I think they just grew apart," said Carol, carefully.

Mary seemed to accept this without comment much to Carol's relief.

"I want to go back to the subject of the keys. Can you think of anyone else who might have a copy and used them."

Mary shrugged. "I can't think of anyone else."

"Not your parents?"

"They're dead."

"Oh I'm sorry to hear that," said Carol awkwardly. Feeling she may have put her foot in it.

"It was a long time ago before Bethany was born."

"What about Jez?"

"His parents? He's never mentioned them at all, so I don't know. They never came to our wedding."

"And you never thought to ask?"

"No, it never occurred to me," said Mary feeling slightly foolish.

It seemed odd to Carol but she decided not to pursue it as she didn't know much about the relationship between Mary and Jez. She didn't know if they knew anything about each others past or if it had all been about the present. It seemed a bit weird to Carol.

"Do you think Jez could have given Anne-Marie a key at all, or could she have discovered it with Jez's keys and decided to copy it.?"

"Why would she do that?" asked Mary confused.

"I don't know. Maybe she wanted to know more about you and if you were a threat to their relationship I don't know."

"I've never met her. I don't know anything about her so can't answer that."

Carol nodded, unsurprised. In fact Mary seemed incredibly naïve about everything. It seemed she lived in a little bubble and saw nothing wrong with anything. A make believe world where everything was perfect and no bad things happened. This worried Carol because she felt Mary would not cope with the reality of what they were discovering. She was starting to sense that Mary was indeed innocent of any wrong doing where Bethany was concerned.

Carol's phone rang, interrupting her thoughts. It was Adam.

"I must take this outside," she said to Mary.

Mary nodded and Carol went outside, shutting the front door behind her. She didn't want Mary overhearing any part of the conversation.

"Hello Adam."

"Hi, are you able to talk."

"Yes. I'm outside with the door shut."

"Good. Firstly Mr Stubbs is insisting he knows nothing about the allegations that have been made against him."

"Well we know that's not true. I can't see six year old children making it up somehow. They are too innocent at that age – or should be. Also Mary has confirmed Bethany didn't like Mr Stubbs and would try to get out of going to school on those days. Mary though doesn't see any wrong in him as he always seems to really care about the children."

"He would, he's a paedophile. We just have to prove it."

"Is he linked to Bethany's disappearance do you think?"

"Not sure, we haven't approached him on that yet. Thanks for telling me about Bethany though as it gives us at least two children that we know about."

"Hey, I've just had an idea!" exclaimed Carol, getting quite excited. "We know he threatens the children not to say anything, you don't think Bethany threatened to tell so he had to carry it out?"

"But it's what all abusers say to keep their victim under control, so I'm not sure it would mean much. Plus Bethany would be too frightened to do that the same as Maddy was. She isn't old enough to realise she could use it to her advantage and manipulate the situation."

"You've got a point," said Carol, deflated.

"We'll go back in with the extra information. Maybe we'll get him to give himself away somehow."

Carol disconnected the call and went back to Mary. She decided not to say anything as yet until she heard anything positive. Also she didn't know whether Mary, on hearing about the abuse would become a one person vigilante and go and confront Mr Stubbs himself. This would undo all the work they were trying to do.

"Was there any indication that Jez might like little girls?" asked Carol.

"What do you mean? I've always said he showed no interest in Beth. He refused to discuss the possibility of having a second child which I wanted."

"Could it be that in that relationship he didn't want to put himself in danger of being found out so he ignored her. He wouldn't have wanted you to find out. Paedophiles can be very clever."

Mary blanched, " Paed…..paedophile?"

Carol realised just how naïve Mary was. It hadn't occurred to her that all the photos Jez had hidden of little girls naked might mean something sinister.

"Yes, Mary," said Carol proceeding more gently. "We believe those photos are of little girls who have been abused by these men."

"But Jez wouldn't. He's not like that."

"How can you be sure. He didn't tell you anything about his past life before he met you so how can you be so sure he hasn't kept other things from you as well. He wouldn't want this particular secret told."

Mary shook her head. "I don't believe it."

"It's all right," said Carol trying to think of a way of changing the subject, at the same time wondering if Mary was hiding something herself. She had a feeling Mary was keeping something back. She had no proof though and didn't know what it could be so held off confronting Mary.

Chapter Seven

The team were sat in the CID office discussing the case. Carol and Adam were still part of the investigation even though it had been passed to detectives now. Carol as family liaison was important and because it concerned very vulnerable people it was thought Adam might still be useful as he knew the case and the people concerned knew him.

Carol was talking, telling the team what she knew so far. There were a few headshakes at Mary's apparent naivety.

"I'm sure she's hiding something important but I don't know what."

"Have you confronted her?" a voice from the back of the room called out.

"No," said Carol. "I can't do that without evidence because I need to keep Mary on side. I have no idea what it could be so can't afford to say anything that is pure guess work at present."

Carol sat back down having finished presenting the latest information from her end.

Adam stood up and talked about his interview with Mr Stubbs. "We are getting nowhere on the case so far. He continues to deny all knowledge of photos with naked small girls. We've tried confronting him saying we have heard from two girls, but he still refuses to say anything. We've offered him a solicitor but he has declined saying he doesn't need one. In my opinion we need to find Jez quickly. Maybe Stubbs would be more open if we found Jez and are able to get something out of him or his girlfriend Anne-Marie."

"Do you think Anne-Marie knows anything."

Adam shrugged, "It's possible but we have no proof of that. Certainly he would have had to make some excuse as to why they should leave so suddenly."

"Could he have just said he'd booked a romantic holiday."

"Possibly," said Adam but probably not. "It's hard to say though with any certainty because we don't know either of them. That's why we have to make finding them a matter of urgency, but that's my opinion."

"I agree," said Detective Sergeant Macintosh. "Why don't you and Carol go and see what you can find out from that nosey neighbour. She might just know a favourite place they like to go. Speak also to his ex boss who might know the same details. If we have an idea of location we'll have a better idea of tracking them down and interviewing them."

Carol and Adam nodded and stood up to leave.

"How are we going to play this?" asked Carol as Adam drove them to Jez's last known address.

"We'll try there first in case they have arrived back in the last few days. If not we'll knock the neighbour up and see what more she can remember."

....

"Well here goes," said Adam as they closed the car doors ready to see if Jez and Anne-Marie were back yet.

Carol pressed her finger on the door bell and left it there. She didn't want to risk them not answering. Adam was stood back a bit, observing the windows to see any twitch in the curtain. There was none.

"Come on," said Adam, "There's no one in. Let's go next door."

They retreated down the path and in at next door's gate. They rang the bell and waited. Nothing. They waited longer to give the elderly woman time to get to the door. This paid off as they heard a shuffling coming from inside moving towards the door.

"Who is it?" asked a quivering voice. The door was open slightly but still on the latch.

Carol and Adam looked at each other. This hadn't been their experience last time.

"We're PCs Witts and Jones," said Carol through the crack in the door. She took Adams id and her own and showed it to Mrs Murray.

"Just a minute."

They waited while the door was shut again and the chain taken off. Mrs Murray cautiously looked around before opening the door wide and letting them in.

Carol gasped as she was about to thank Mrs Murray.

Her face was black and blue with one eye swollen shut and the other was bloodshot and only open a slit.

"What happened?" asked Carol gently.

It was obviously the older lady had been beaten.

Mrs Murray shook her head. She was obviously scared by the look on her face and didn't want to say anything. She swayed slightly causing Carol to quickly take an arm and usher her through to the living room where Mrs Murray sank gratefully into an armchair.

"Now can you tell us what happened?" asked Adam.

"The doorbell rang a couple of days after I last saw you. I went to answer it as usual when him from next door...." She paused.

"You mean Jez?" asked Carol in the silence.

Mrs Murray nodded her head, wincing with the pain.

"What happened next?" asked Adam gently.

"He, he pushed his way in and put his hands around my throat pinning me against the wall. He threatened me to stop me from speaking to you. He then proceeded to pummel his fist into my face telling me if I spoke to you again he'd kill me."

"I'm so sorry if we brought that upon you. How did he know you'd spoken to us when he was away?" asked Carol.

"He said someone had told him. He said he had spies everywhere."

"Can you tell us if they are at home now and when we might find them in?" asked Adam.

"Later I think. I saw them go out about an hour ago."

"Thanks you've been very helpful. One more thing however. Do you by any chance notice anyone going regularly next door."

Mrs Murray paused before answering, lost in thought. She wanted to be sure she was giving the correct information. It was in spite of the threats and the beating she still wanted to help the police all she could.

She nodded, saying, "One man, quite short and tubby."

"Anything else?" queried Carol. She and Adam exchanged glances. The description sounded just like Mr Stubbs the art teacher.

"No sorry."

"How often does he come and what time of day."

"A couple of times a week I should think."

"Have you spoken to him?"

Mrs Murray shook her head. I usually withdraw my face from the window if I see him glance in this direction. He looks a nasty piece of work and I want nothing to do with him." She paused before adding, "Maybe it was him that told Jez I'd been talking to you."

"It's certainly possible," said Adam. "You are doing the right thing by avoiding him and thanks for having the courage to speak to us. Your information is valuable. It can't have been easy though."

"Have you seen a doctor about those injuries?" asked Carol.

Mrs Murray shook her head once again. "Don't see much point it's only severe bruising that will take time to go down completely."

"I think you should see a doctor. We can drop you at minor injuries."

Mrs Murray shook her head. "I don't want you to go out of your way for a silly fool like me."

"You're not a silly fool," said Carol. "You're a decent human being who has got into more than you'd prefer."

Mrs Murray nodded. "I agree if that's all right. I know I should have got checked out at the time but fear stopped me."

"Come on then we'll get you there safely don't worry about that."

In the car Mrs Murray obviously relaxed. She felt safer now but she knew the anxiety would creep back in when she was home again. She was grateful for all the officers had done for her but knew she had to keep things to herself to avoid being punched all over again. She was under no illusion, Jez would kill her if necessary. She wasn't ready to die just yet.

Arriving at the hospital Carol helped Mrs Murray in. It was Carol that booked her in and waited until she was called.

"You don't have to wait for me. It could be hours yet. You can see how busy it is in here."

It was very busy, Carol acknowledged, but wasn't deterred. She felt it best to stay with the older woman. She quickly sent a text to Adam to let him know her plans so he didn't have to sit there all day. He responded to say he'd go in and wait as well. It would be useful to see what the doctor said as he was keen to charge Jez with assault given the opportunity. Also they would be needing a lift back home and he didn't think it safe for Mrs Murray to be on her own even if it were in a taxi.

Adam went to find somewhere to park then joined the two women in the hospital. Before going in he had radioed through to the station to let them know where they were and what was happening.

He gave Carol a nod over Mrs Murray's head to indicate what he had done. Carol used to such gestures knew straight away what he meant and that the station had agreed to them staying there.

They sat in silence not wanting to say anything about the investigation for others to here. As it was they were getting wary looks from those around them. Probably the sight of Mrs Murray's face and the uniformed officers sat either side of her.

As time went by Carol started to get bored and wished she'd taken a book with her. She was easily bored and needing something to do. As an avid reader she always carried her kindle with her. It was nice to be able to keep it in her bag to pull out when needed. She loved her kindle as it enabled to have a library of books wherever she went. She didn't know how she had forgotten to put it in her bag. She was grateful to the inventor of it.

"I'm going to see how much longer we're going to be," said Adam.

He stood up and went to the reception to find out. He had a whispered conversation with the receptionist. Nodding, he went back to the two women.

"We're next," he said. What he didn't say was that he had managed to get them bumped to the top of the queue, using his status as a busy officer who was needed back at work.

It was just another five minutes before they were called by a young female doctor. She couldn't have been in the job very long. She blanched when she saw Mrs Murray having never seen such a beating before. Not wanting to seem as new as she was she quickly pulled herself together and led the way to a cubicle.

"Right what's happened here?" she asked.

It was left to Carol to explain as Mrs Murray sat in silence in awe of the young doctor's brusque manner. The doctor started to feel around Mrs Murray's face without a word. She decided nothing was broken just bad bruising but she ordered x-rays just in case. They came back clear and Mrs Murray was sent home with pain killers and told it would be sometime before the bruising faded.

Mrs Murray was relieved to be back in the car going home. "I didn't like that doctor's manner," she said.

Carol responded, "She was very young. I bet she was new to the job. She probably feels intimidated by all the patients and their different ailments. She could have adopted that manner to avoid getting too involved and to make herself more competent and in control than she actually felt."

Mrs Murray nodded uncertainly. She wasn't convinced. "I'd much rather see a male doctor," she said. She was old school and thought being a doctor was a male occupation. Nursing was for the female species.

"We have to move with the times," commented Carol.

"I'm a bit too old for that dearie," said the older woman. "In my day these young'uns would show respect not beat up a defenceless old woman."

Carol and Adam nodded.

Adam said, "Bring back whipping and hanging then that Jez can really be punished."

"Agree 100%," said Mrs Murray. "Someone on my wavelength at least."

Carol and Adam exchanged glances in the rear view mirror and Carol nodded. In future it would be left to Adam to do the questioning if they needed to speak to Mrs Murray further. He definitely had made a connection with her.

Finally back Adam, ever the gentleman, helped Mrs Murray out of the car and into her own home. He insisted on sitting her down comfortably then went to the kitchen to make some tea for her. After this he bade his farewell and left her.

Back at the car they decided once more to try next door to see if they were to get any response this time.

"There has to be someone in. They can't stay out permanently surely," said Carol in frustration. "It feels as if this investigation is on hold while we wait for them to be in."

"I don't suppose they are staying somewhere nearby, thinking we won't find them," said Adam.

Carol looked despondent at this, saying, "Don't say that, we'll never find them if that's the case."

"What about trying that Mr Stubbs again? He might be persuaded to tell us if he knows."

Carol looked dubious and said, "He hasn't been very cooperative so far."

"I know but you never know he might if he thinks an older lady has been badly assaulted. I'll call it into the station and see what they say."

After a few minutes he was off the phone and said, "The DS says we can give it a go as we've nothing to lose."

Carol nodded and turned the car around to go back in the direction the teacher lived. They knew he wouldn't be at work as he had been suspended pending investigation after the allegations had been made.

Carol rang the bell while Adam watched for signs of life. It wasn't long before the door was opened.

"Not you again," he said. "You're not welcome here. I've lost my job because of you lot. I want adequate compensation for the trouble you've caused me."

"You know very well you're guilty. Anyway we've come about Jez and Anne Marie," said Adam.

"I don't know anyone of that name."

"We think you do because the photos came from Jez's house."

"So you say. I still say I don't know them."

"An older lady has been attacked by Jez."

"So! I wasn't involved with that. I don't beat up old ladies." Mr Stubbs looked quite put out.

"No you prefer little girls," sneered Adam. "We're interested in this Jez you say you don't know. He has been identified as the attacker and we think you may know his whereabouts."

"What if I do know something, he'll come after me next. If he can do that to an old lady then he'll do worse to me."

"Look do you really want to have this pointless conversation on your doorstep or shall we go inside."

Mr Stubbs sighed and stood away from the door so they could go in.

The two officers looked around curiously. They found the house dark and dingy. The curtains were still closed in the living room and newspapers were all over the place along with two full ash trays and the smell of cigarettes filling the air. Carol wrinkled her nose. She was sensitive to smell and cigarettes was one she couldn't stand at all. Mr Stubbs noticed and smirked.

"If you don't like it we can go outside again. It's not as if I want you in."

He made no attempt to find space for them to sit down so they were left standing in the doorway of the living room.

"Ok we only want to know the whereabouts of Jez," said Adam.

"Who says I know anything."

Adam sighed. "Look we're not here to play games. We just want to know where to find him then we'll be out of your way."

"Why don't you try his home. That seems logical." Mr Stubbs was determined to be unhelpful.

"We've been there and he hasn't been seen at that address for a while."

"You could always try his wife. He could be there considering his daughter has gone missing. Cute she was. I sincerely hope you find her."

"What do you mean, cute?"

"Exactly what I say."

"Hmm."

Carol and Adam exchanged looks and Carol gave an imperceptible nod.

"Ok. We're leaving you but we'll be back if we draw blank. So don't even think of messing us about. We still want to know what you mean by cute but that can wait. We're more concerned with finding Jez at the moment."

"Bye bye," said the teacher.

"I wanted to wring his neck. He was mocking us," said Adam as they got in the car.

"I know what you mean. We'll get him, we just have to be careful," said Carol.

Chapter Eight

"Hello Mary," said Carol. "We need to ask you some questions which may seem a bit strange to you right now. We just need to eliminate something."

Mary nodded but her eyes looked warily from one officer to the other. "I'll help if I can."

"Has Jez been in touch at all?" asked Carol.

Mary paled alarmingly.

Carol stood up and went to stand by Mary's chair and held her arm. "Are you all right?"

"I…I don't know. Why would you ask such a question when you know we have no contact and he didn't even want to know when Beth went missing."

"I know but we were given some information that led us to believe he was hiding here possibly with his latest girlfriend Anne Marie."

"That's not true. I've not heard anything from him and he certainly isn't here. If you don't believe me you can look around."

"That's all right we don't need to go that far. We just had to verify it that's all. We need to find him as a matter of urgency."

"Well how do you expect me to know?" asked Mary with an edge to her voice. "What's he done this time.?"

"I'm afraid we can't discuss that. It isn't directly to do with Beth though. It's related to another matter which suddenly came up."

Mary shrugged.

Carol looked at Adam. This was not going too well at all. They had never seen this side to Mary before and they could only hope that it wouldn't damage the relationship built up when it came to Beth. There was a hardness in her voice. It seemed as if there were going to have to be bridges built again. It was a giant step backwards and would require some effort to get back to the same footing.

"Ok, if you can't help we'll leave you in peace for now. Carol will be back later."

Carol nodded to confirm this.

"Don't bother unless you've something positive to tell me," said Mary dismissively.

……..

"Oh dear that went well I don't think," said Carol.

"It certainly did but I think we did learn something from it which could be important, you never know."

"Like what?"

"Well, we know Mary isn't the gentle, heartbroken person who had fallen to pieces."

"You're right I hadn't thought of that. It was a whole different side to her which somehow takes away some of her innocence."

Adam nodded. "It could make a big difference with the way we look at the case."

"But it still leaves me with some building of bridges to do between her and us."

"Yes but it could make it easier to get some answers from her if she isn't crumbling inside. We can approach her differently."

"Come on then, we can't sit here all day. We should get back to the station and report back on what has been going on."

………

Mary watched them go. She still couldn't work out what had been going on and it made her uneasy. Why should they come to her to look for Jez it didn't make sense. Hadn't she been through enough with her Beth going missing. Did they suspect her of having some involvement in some way? She hoped not. She loved Beth and missed her with her whole heart.

She checked her watch and decided to give Liz a call. Maybe she'd be available to meet up for a cuppa before going to the school.

"Ok but I can't come to you. Can we meet up in town outside M&S?" asked Liz when Mary phoned her.

"No problem I'll be about fifteen minutes."

Mary rushed to put her shoes on and went straight out to the car, only having to go back indoors for her bag which had her keys in. She shook her head. She'd always been so organised but now her head was all over the place.

……….

Mary looked around, starting to get a bit agitated and not knowing what to do. Liz wasn't there despite agreeing to meet up. Had there been a misunderstanding? Mary had got there as soon as she could. She had only been a few minutes late so Liz could have waited for her.

"Sorry," said Liz as she rushed breathlessly up to Mary.

Mary's face relaxed into a slight smile.

"You all right," asked Liz. She knew her friend inside out and could read every nuance in her face.

Mary shook her head.

"Come on let's go and get that drink then we can chat," said Liz taking the mute Mary by the arm.

It was only when they were sat in the café sipping the hot tea that Mary started to relax and tell Liz what had happened with the police.

"But they weren't accusing you of anything were they?"

Mary shook her head, "I don't think so."

"Well then, they were just following the trail which they hoped would lead to Jez."

"But why think he was with me when they know what happened between us. They must have known I'm still desperate to find my daughter."

"They know. While they suspect Jez of some involvement they have to follow every lead even if it leads to a dead end."

"How come you know so much?" asked Mary, surprised at her friend's knowledge.

"I used to go out with a policeman many years ago."

"You never told me," said Mary a bit put out.

"I did, don't you remember?"

Mary sat quietly, lost in thought, She thought she knew everything about her friend but it seemed she was keeping secrets from her. Liz knew everything there was to know about Mary so why hold back about her own life. Was it possible that the voice on the phone was telling the truth and Liz was involved and knew something.

"Earth to Mary," said Liz, her voice sounding a long way off to Mary.

Mary shook her head to clear it of the intrusive and unwelcome thoughts.

"You all right?" asked Liz in some concern.

"Yes fine. Still thinking about the police that's all," lied Mary. For some reason she didn't want Liz to know what she had been thinking. Instinct she supposed. She always prided herself on her instincts which were usually good. This time however she seemed to have got everything mixed up. What else could she have got so wrong she wondered.

Mary suddenly paled, jumped to her feet and ran out of the small café they were sat in.

"Hey what's wrong? Where are you going?" called Liz concerned. Her friend seemed to be losing the plot a bit, not that she could blame her she had a lot to contend with.

Liz was just in time to see Mary grab hold of a young girl who was just about to get on the roundabout.

"Hey what do you think you're doing?" said a woman trying to get Mary away from the girl.

"It's Beth, my Beth coming back to me."

"Come on Mary, let's get away from here," said Liz arriving at the scene. "It's not Beth."

"But I thought……"

"Sorry," said Liz to the woman. "She just lost her daughter. She doesn't know what she's doing."

"She's a loony, not fit to be out on the streets," said the woman holding her daughter close to her.

"Come on Mary let's get you home."

Mary was sat on the pavement head in hands. She had just made a giant fool of herself, enough to be getting funny looks from the people who had been near enough to see what had happened.

Liz leaned down to take Mary's hand to help her up. Mary resisted it though. She couldn't face going home one little bit. It was too quiet without Beth running around playing. Mary sometimes got fed up of Beth's constant energy but longed for Beth to be back causing trouble as always. To feel Beth's smooth, perfect skin against her. Her lovely shoulder length hair, so silky and golden in this sun. Her Beth! Would she ever see her again?

Liz broke into Mary's reverie, bringing her back to the present and the reality broke in. She burst into loud sobs which drew more attention to the two women.

"Come on, let's get you home now," said Liz, repeating herself. "I'll collect your car for you later."

Mary looked up at her best friend with no recognition in her dull, teary eyes. She didn't resist when Liz put her arm around her and helped her stand. Slowly Liz and Mary made their way back to Mary's house.

Once there Liz made Mary a cup of hot, sweet tea. When Mary was slowly sipping it Liz left, unable to stay with her friend any longer. She made a mental note to ring the liaison officer dealing with the case. She must also check up on Mary the next day.

Chapter Nine

Carol and Adam were on their way to Jez's place of employment until he was dismissed.

Matthew didn't look pleased to see them when the receptionist showed them through.

"Yes?" he queried in an abrupt manner.

"We're wondering if you could tell us anymore about Jez's whereabouts. It's imperative we find him. We need to talk to him about several matters," said Adam, taking the lead as discussed in the car. It was felt Matthew might be likely to respond better if it were male to male. Carol stood their taking notes and observing the situation.

"Sorry I can't help you. I told you everything I know the other day."

"We may need to search your house to satisfy ourselves that you are telling the truth. If you're withholding information and we discover this you are liable to be charged with wasting police time."

Carol left the room and called through for advice. She went back in to tell the men a search warrant was being applied for to search the work premises as well as Matthew's house.

"It's not that we don't believe you," said Adam waving his hand at Matthew's protestations. "But this is a matter of some urgency. A little girl's life is at stake here. The longer she goes without being found the worse the outcome. That's our experience."

Carol nodded in agreement.

Adam and Carol stayed close to Matthew whilst waiting for the search warrants to be obtained. They weren't even letting him go to the loo on his own in case he tried to contact Jez.

"This is totally ridiculous," cried Matthew as Adam insisted on taking his mobile while escorting him to the loo.

"Just taking precautions sir," said Adam.

The warrant came through in an hour and Adam and Carol began searching the work premises and speaking to other employees. No one seemed to know anything and possessed no interest or liking for Jez.

Nothing was found. There were no links to Jez on the computer either. Other staff on questioning showed no love was lost on Jez. He had definitely not been a popular person amongst the others which fitted the profile they were building.

……..

"You won't find anything," said Matthew.

"You may as well cooperate with us as we'll find anything there is to find," said Adam.

"I've got nothing to hide"

"Maybe not but we have to look. It seems Jez is not at home but he has to be staying somewhere local as he made threats to someone."

"He always was a bit of a hot head. He never threatened his wife though. She was never at risk nor his child. He preferred to pretend she wasn't there. Sad really."

They took Matthew home in the police car. They didn't want to risk him alerting anyone if he knew where Jez was and was covering for him.

Nothing was found at the house either. It was dull and dark inside. A typical bachelor pad. They were surprised he wasn't married, someone of his age and asked about it.

"I'm separated," said Matthew when questioned. "No children. I am seeing someone though who has a child. I love kids especially when they are really young. There's an innocence about them don't you think."

Carol and Adam looked at each other and Carol raised her eyebrows. Was it possible they had stumbled across another member of the paedophile ring.

Matthew noticed their look and said, "I'm not like that you know. It's a normal feeling that most people have about children that's all."

"How do you know what we were thinking as we said nothing?"

"It was the look that passed between you both."

"Hmm."

"I think you need to accompany us back to the station to answer more questions."

"Why? I haven't done anything," protested Matthew.

"You haven't got anything to worry about then have you," stated Adam.

Matthew gave in, seeing he wasn't going to get far with them unless he cooperated.

………

"Right this is for the tape. Matthew can you look through these photos and tell us if you recognise anyone or anything strikes you as odd."

Matthew began looking, getting paler as he looked. "This is atrocious. All very young girls. I assume this is connected to paedophiles. I think I'm going to be sick."

Adam and Carol looked at each other. Was this genuine or was he just a good actor?

Matthew started retching. Carol taking a chance said, "Ok there's no need for the theatrics. We get the message."

"I'm being serious," he said before being sick all over the floor.

"Ok interview terminated at 15.30 hours," said Adam.

"I'll see if another room is free that we can continue in while the cleaners clear up this," said Carol looking at the vomit in disgust.

It wasn't long before they began again, this time in another interview room.

"Where did you find these photos? They really are gross," asked Matthew.

"That's none of your business."

"I'm not like this, really I'm not."

The two officers were starting to think this was for real. Matthew really did seem genuine in his disgust. He seemed completely surprised by the photos and knew nothing of where they had come from. After an hour they let him go. They clearly weren't going to get anymore information out of him. They just hoped they were right in their judgement.

....

"Nothing sir, we drew a blank with Matthew. He's innocent I'm sure of it," said Adam when he reported back to CID.

The detective sergeant nodded and gave a grunt. "So are we any further forward in finding this Jez character?"

"No sir," said Adam.

"Maybe you should get back to the house in case he turns up there."

"How long do you want us to stay there?" asked Carol.

"The rest of the shift would be good."

"But I really need to get to Mary again."

"This is more pressing somehow," said the DS.

Adam and Carol nodded. They had to do as they were told whether they liked it or not.

Chapter Ten

It was time for the outing Mary had planned but she was wary of Liz. She'd had enough of her friend the day before. She was feeling a bit worried. She longed to tell Carol what her thoughts were but hadn't seen her for a while. She knew she could ring her at any time but she felt like a time waster if she did.

The doorbell rang. Mary still got her hopes up every time and felt extreme disappointed when it wasn't Beth. She knew it would be Liz but still had her hopes up. The look on her face when she saw her friend was too much for Liz who was starting to get impatient. Why couldn't she just get on with her life? It was very boring listening to the same broken record all the time.

"Come on then, where shall we go today?" asked Liz, unable to keep the brusque tone from her voice.

"I don't care," said Mary, her watery, red eyes telling their own story.

"Ok why don't we go to the National Trust property. We always get a nice cup of tea there. It's a nice day so we can have a wander round the grounds and relax. No hurry."

"But...."

"No buts," said Liz breaking in not wanting to hear the rest of the sentence. It was bound to be about Beth.

"I'm not sure about this."

"You misery guts it'll be good for you. You need to get on with your life. You can't continue living as if Beth will turn up any minute. She's gone, accept it. Don't turn on the waterworks please," said Liz seeing that Mary was crying again.

Mary hastily sniffed and dried her eyes with a sodden tissue. Why was it that people didn't like to see pain in others even when they were supposed to be your best friend? She was also discovering her other friends were ignoring her. Liz was the only one still sticking by her and now she was growing cold. She assumed it must be because people didn't know what to say. Also to hear someone's misery meant they were just as fallible and bad things could happen to them.

Liz drove in silence, not knowing what to say to her friend anymore. "Look I'm sorry for the way I spoke to you. I know you're struggling to cope. To be honest I don't know what to say to make it better."

"You don't have to say anything. Just be my friend."

"I'll try but be patient with me when I get it wrong. I don't really want to lose your friendship."

Mary nodded, unsure herself how to respond to this apology. All she really wanted to do was talk about Beth but it seemed that subject was off limits. She needed to keep Beth alive in her mind, she couldn't just let her go it would be like admitting she didn't think she would ever see her daughter alive again and that was an impossibility. She would never stop hoping even when she was an elderly lady at the end of her life.

They arrived at the property and got out of the car. They were still awkward with each other as if they were mere acquaintances instead of close friends. They were each trying to avoid the topic of children.

…………..

They walked along in companionable silence as Liz felt Mary start to relax beside her. This outing was obviously a good idea after all. Get Mary away from the familiar environment was allowing Mary some space to sort her head out.

"Shall we go to the café now. I could just do with a good cuppa," said Liz.

Mary nodded, lost in thought. Unbeknown to Liz Mary's thoughts were still consumed with Beth and she was looking around at every young child wondering if she would see hers. There seemed to be a party of school children there about Beth's age. Mary was paying close attention to them. Maybe, just maybe, one of them was Beth. Then she saw her. Forgetting Liz she rushed over shouting Beth's name. No one turned round at the voice in fact some of the children were starting to cry, frightened by the strange lady approaching calling a name.

Mary reached out to the child she believed to be her daughter and swung her round. It wasn't Beth. Tears of disappointment slid down her face. Liz realising what was happening a bit too late came rushing forward. She grabbed Mary's arm and pulled her away from the group just as a teacher started shouting at Mary and threatening to call the police.

"Don't do that. My friend has just lost a child about the same age as the children here. She can't let her daughter go," said Liz.

"I'm sorry if that's the case but I still have a responsibility for these children to keep them safe. I have no choice but to report it," said the teacher, getting her phone out of her bag and pressing some numbers.

Liz grabbed Mary's arm saying, "Come on let's get out of here. You're really in trouble this time and I doubt I can talk them out of it. This has to stop you know. I'm not always going to be around to talk you out of trouble. You need to move on, forget Beth. If you want a child find yourself a boyfriend and try for a baby."

Mary gasped. "How could you be so cruel. You're supposed to be my friend."

"I am your friend," replied Liz. "That's why I'm telling you this. I hate to see you torturing yourself."

"It was you," cried Mary out of the blue. "You took Beth. You've got a key. I forgot you had a key when the police were asking."

"What are you talking about? Of course I haven't taken Beth. You're deluded."

"It must be you. That's why you're speaking like this. You're a traitor." Mary's anger rose in her and she snatched her arm away from Liz and rushed on ahead.

Liz stood looking after her in disbelief.

"Mary, come back and stop this nonsense. You don't know what you're saying. Come on let's change the subject and pretend this conversation never happened," called Liz to no avail. Mary continued striding ahead without looking back.

Sirens could be heard in the distance getting closer all the time. The police turned up moments later.

"Ok what's all this about."

The teacher spoke first, not giving Liz an opportunity to say anything.

"Where is the lady now?" asked the officer.

"She ran off after an argument with her friend," the teacher responded. "She's a lunatic. Should be locked up if you ask me," she said completely unsympathetic to Mary's plight.

"Do you know where she might have gone?" asked the officer turning to Liz.

"No, not really. We were talking about going to the café when she thought she saw her daughter. I'm really sorry but my friend is going through a difficult time at the moment. She isn't fully aware of her actions."

"Ok we'll start with the café. If you could accompany us so you can identify your friend."

Liz nodded and started walking down the path to the café. She didn't really expect to find Mary there. That would be stupid of her if she needed to get away by herself and avoid trouble with the police. Sure enough Mary was not anywhere to be seen. Liz even asked the staff in the café if her friend had been in, only to be met with a shake of her head.

The police looked at Liz for guidance. "Sorry I have no idea where she might be. She ran off in this direction. I'm afraid I may have upset her so she would be avoiding me as well. I wasn't very nice to her."

"That's not very helpful," said the officer. "Where does she live? Could she have just gone home on her own."

Liz shook her head. "We came in my car so no."

"Can we go to the car park, maybe she'll be there waiting for you."

"It seems a long shot, she won't want to be near me but we can try."

Exactly as Liz had said Mary was not there.

"Where now?" asked the officer who had been taking the lead since their arrival.

Liz shrugged, having no idea and not sure she wanted to say anything either. After all, Mary was still her friend, or at least she hoped so and she didn't want her in trouble. She was already going through too much. It wasn't really surprising that the events had tipped her over the edge. No one knew how they would react in such a situation.

"Are you sure you can't think of anywhere else?" asked the officer suspiciously.

Liz shook her head.

"Could she have gone home maybe?"

"Unlikely. It's too far to walk."

"What about catching a bus?"

"I don't even know where the bus stop would be or which bus would take us home. We always come by car."

"What's her address we can try there. We need to speak to her to ensure she doesn't do this again. We need to make sure she is safe around other children. We don't want other children going missing."

"She would never take a child!" exclaimed Liz, horrified on Mary's behalf.

"Who knows how she would react in such a situation."

"She wouldn't. I know her, we're best friends."

"Not close enough friends that would stop her running off like that without telling you where she was going."

"We'd argued. She accused me of taking her daughter away from her. She was just lashing out in anger. She didn't mean it."

"So again I query how close you really are. Surely if you were that close she would know you wouldn't have done such a thing and you would have some ideas as to where she could be now."

"We are and that's the truth. We both said some hurtful things. I became impatient with her and said to forget her daughter and move on."

"That doesn't sound like the words of a close friend," observed the officer.

"I know and I'm really ashamed of myself now," said Liz blushing furiously.

"Well I suppose we'd better go to her address to see if she's gone home. You can drive your own car but PC Browning will accompany you so you can't send a message to alert her to our presence."

"I doubt she'll answer me."

"We can't take that risk. You could be sending us on a wild goose chase for all we know. You could know where she is if she is hiding waiting for you to say the coast is clear."

"I can't lie to you. You're the police."

"That means nothing. People lie to us all the time. We assume people are lying until we prove they are telling the truth."

"Not me," stated Liz firmly.

They drove to the address Liz gave them. Liz drove in silence not wanting to engage in conversation with PC Browning who was by her side in the passenger seat.

They soon reached Mary's house. The officer whom Liz privately thought as a cynical bully rung the bell and kept his finger on it. No answer.

"She wouldn't have got home yet if she was on the bus."

"How do you know when you say you know nothing about the buses."

"It's common sense. Buses stop and start and she would have had to have taken two buses. One from there to the bus station and a second one out to here."

"Let's say you're right and that's what she's done she'll still turn up here eventually. We can't wait at every stop just in case she's on the bus when we don't even know for sure that's what she's done."

"Do you know of any other place she could have gone?"

Liz thought for a while before saying, "The park I suppose. We go there a lot. We both have good memories of that time."

"Have you been there recently?"

Liz nodded. "She saw a child there as well whom she thought was Beth."

"So this isn't the first time she's done this then?"

Liz could have kicked herself. She didn't want to drop Mary in it and it seemed that was what she may have done.

She sighed before saying, "Why don't you leave and I'll wait here until she gets back and I can persuade her to come here and make a statement."

"How do you expect us to believe that when you are at great pains to tell us you had an argument ."

"I really don't know what to think anymore. You're confusing me."

"Hmm. That's our job. It's how we get to the truth of what people are saying, by confusing them. It's hard to keep up a lie when questions are frequently being pushed at a topic."

"You must be successful at it as you have certainly muddled me, until I feel I don't know what truth is anymore."

PC Browning couldn't hide the smile at this comment. It was just where his colleague excelled. Quite often it led to revelations and the truth coming out except on this occasion. It seemed like he had met his match well and truly here.

The officer concerned also felt this and was somehow convinced that Liz knew more than she was saying. There was something fishy here he could sniff it out a mile off.

Liz wasn't happy at being accused of God knows what but she knew deep down she deserved it, she hadn't been as forthcoming as she could have been.

"I really believe she would try and make her way back here. It's the only logical thing she could have done."

"In my opinion people don't always react logical when wanted by us."

"But Mary has nothing to hide."

"Hasn't she. She approached a strange child and grabbed them in a public place."

Liz nodded, not knowing what else to say. She had run out of words. Anyway she couldn't win he always had something to say in return. She was very defensive of her friend.

Liz saw her before anyone else did. When Mary saw the three stood at the door she turned around and went in the other direction. She really didn't want to see the police or her so called friend. She had calmed down on the journey home but seeing Liz still brought up a lot of negative feelings in her. She honestly didn't know if they could get their friendship back on track. It would be a long time before she could forgive Liz for those words that had hurt so deep within.

Liz kept quiet wanting to give her friend time to get away.

After a few minutes she said, "That was her."

She pointed in the direction Mary had gone a short while before. PC Browning was the fastest and almost caught up with her but not quite. There was something in him that felt protective of the woman he knew they needed to talk to. It wasn't until his colleague joined him that they had to accepted they had lost her. Going back to Liz who had stayed behind at the house they insisted she call them the minute she turned up.

Liz nodded but didn't say a word. What a mess this whole situation was. Mary had been through enough without her betrayal on top. How she regretted her words spoken in the heat of the moment out of embarrassment more than anything.

Liz followed in the direction Mary had gone hoping to find her. She knew she didn't deserve it but she needed to apologise to Mary and hoped she would accept it. How had life got so messed up? She thought she saw her friend in the distance and called to her. Mary half turned before hurrying on the way she was going. Liz called again but was ignored. Giving up Liz turned back and got in her car to drive home, hoping that Mary would be in contact again soon.

Chapter Eleven

Mary answered the door as expectant as ever. Her jaw dropped when she saw it was Carol looking unusually serious.

Mary stood aside to let her in without a word. She wasn't in the mood for Carol or anyone. She just wanted to be left alone with her thoughts.

"We need a chat," said Carol. "I heard what happened yesterday."

"I'm sorry, I know it was wrong of me it's just she looked so like Beth."

"You can't keep doing that Mary. It's not on. You'll get yourself in serious trouble if you keep doing it. This time I've managed to get you off the hook with Sergeant Macintosh but I won't be able to again."

"You mean they'll leave me alone?"

"Only if you behave yourself and don't approach children again, This is serious Mary. I don't want to see you appear in court charged with something. Beth needs you to be strong and to be there for her when she comes home."

Mary's face brightened momentarily. "You mean you've found her. Is she coming home?"

Carol shook her head, "No news yet."

"Why get my hopes up then. That seems so cruel under the circumstances."

"I wasn't trying to get your hopes up, just pointing out if we do find Beth she'll need you to be there for her not sitting in some prison cell."

"Do you still think you'll find her?"

"There is always hope and you mustn't forget that. We're still working on the case, we haven't given up yet."

What Carol didn't say was that the more time that went by the less chance there was of finding the girl alive. Also there were very few new leads to follow. It didn't help that the abduction was at night from the child's bed so there weren't going to be any witnesses to it, which might have led to something. They had checked the nearby river but nothing.

"Did you find Jez?" asked Mary, thinking back to their last conversation.

"Not yet," said Carol.

It was strange an appeal had gone out and police nationwide were looking out for him. They had no idea where he could be. They were sure he was being hidden somewhere but if he was no one was giving him and Anne Marie away.

"I think you should be looking more at Liz," said Mary before explaining further.

When she had finished telling Carol about that last conversation with Liz she waited for a response.

"It might just have been said in the spur of the moment," said Carol. "She might not have meant any of it. Don't worry though, I'll pass it on but don't get your hopes up."

On that note Carol bade Mary goodbye and left. She was in a hurry to speak to her colleagues about Liz. They hadn't actually questioned Liz as yet, deeming it as unnecessary, after all she was a close friend of Mary. Surely she wouldn't stab her friend in the back like that. Taking a child was serious stuff.

....

Back at the station Carol gave her feedback from her chat with Mary.

"That's interesting. Can you and Adam go and speak to this Liz. We should at least follow it up just in case it leads us somewhere. While you are with her you could try sounding her out about Jez and his possible whereabouts. After all as a close friend of Mary she should know Jez well."

....

"How are we going to play this?" asked Adam whilst on their way to the address they had for Liz.

"I'll take the lead I think. I'll be as sympathetic as I can but if necessary you can come in and take over with the bad cop routine. Hopefully she'll be more likely to respond well to me."

Adam nodded his agreement. It was exactly as he had thought.

Pulling up outside the address they paused before getting out of the car. This was a nice part of the town and this house was no exception. They garden had a border of flowers and plants with a bush in each corner. The house itself was a semi and looked well looked after.

There was a car in the drive giving them hope that they would find Liz at home. They approached the house and Adam pressed the bell briefly. They could hear the loud chimes spread throughout which was also clearly audible to them outside.

The door was soon opened and Liz gave them a smile when she recognised them from when she had been with Mary previously.

"Come in. What do I owe this pleasure?"

The three sat down in the comfortable living room with lovely leather sofas.

Carol got straight down to business and told her what Mary had told her. "So can you tell us of your version of events."

"There isn't much to tell. That's basically what happened."

Carol nodded and glanced at Adam. They didn't think they would get much information here. Liz was very guarded in her words not wanting to say anything that might drop Mary in trouble.

"Mary isn't in trouble this time," said Carol as if she could read Liz's mind.

"She has made an allegation about you though. Could you explain to us why you spoke to Mary like that."

"I'm sorry if you've had a wasted trip but it was just a misunderstanding."

"It doesn't seem that way to us. You seemed very confident that Beth wasn't coming back," said Adam coming into the conversation after he and Carol had exchanged a glance with a slight nod from Carol.

"I just spoke in the spur of the moment. It was impatience nothing more than that really. I'm sorry if you thought anything else. I really can't help you further."

"You might be able to. As a close friend you could have some idea of the whereabouts of Jez."

Liz shrugged saying nothing at first.

"Come on you might as well tell us what you know. It is a matter of urgency that we find him. He is wanted for questioning on something else not just the disappearance of Beth."

"Look I know about the links to paedophilia if that's what you mean."

Adam shook his head. "It's not. We can't say what's happened other than we need to speak to him."

"Well you are wasting your time speaking to me. I know nothing. I haven't seen him or had any contact with him since their marriage broke down."

"How well do you know him."

"Not very. The only contact we had was in passing when I was visiting Mary. If you want the truth I always thought she deserved better, but she couldn't see it, she was so in love with him you see. It was a relief to me when Mary finally saw sense and threw him out. I hadn't been comfortable around him. There was always something creepy about him although I could never put my finger on what was off about him."

"It's easy to say that in hindsight."

"It wasn't just that. I mentioned something to Mary more that once about him, but she wouldn't listen."

"You've got a son haven't you," said Carol entering the conversation again.

"Yes."

"Did you ever have any suspicions about Jez and his alleged liking of young children."

"No it never occurred to me to think that. He was totally against Beth and suggested more than once that they give her up for adoption."

Carol made a note in her note book at that before raising her eyebrows to Adam. This was news to them and might be a possible lead to follow up.

"We're going to leave now. I think that's all we need to know for the moment. We'll be back if we have any further questions.

The three stood up and Liz showed the two officers out.

"Well what did you think of that," asked Carol when they were in the car.

"I'm not sure. She was a bit contradictory. Claiming on the one hand that she didn't know him well and on the other she seemed to know more than she was letting on. She was a bit too cagey for my liking. I don't know where she fits it in to the situation though."

"I agree. I think we need to have another chat with Mary about what Liz has said."

Before they could move off they had a phone call from the CID officers working on the case.

Adam paled as he listened. "Ok thanks for letting us know. We'll be there as soon as we can."

He turned to Carol. "That was Maurice. He said they've found a body in the river about thirty miles away. They think the body drifted somewhat. There is evidence of foul play."

"Beth?" queried Carol.

"I don't know he didn't say anymore than that. Other than to add he wants us there as soon as possible."

Carol nodded and they set off. The conversation with Mary would have to wait.

Chapter Twelve

"I want mummy," cried the little girl.

"Mummy's been naughty so she can't have you. This is the best way to punish her. Now eat this quickly," said the person.

The voice was disguised to avoid Beth being able to recognise them. The person was also wearing a mask. He wore the mask of a clown to ensure Beth wasn't frightened. It wasn't part of the plan to frighten the small child. Later it wouldn't be necessary to use disguises. They would be open with each other and Beth. They would have a new life together as a family but for now things had to be this way. Plans for the future were on going.

Beth ate what she was given and had a drink. She laid back on the coarse blanket which would have irritated her skin normally but she was asleep most of the time. It was necessary as they couldn't risk anyone hearing anything and calling the police. That was definitely not part of the long term plans they had for Beth. It would also make it easier when they moved and revealed themselves properly. Beth would soon get used to her new mummy and daddy and forget her real mother.

The person satisfied that Beth was asleep for the next few hours left the damp, dark basement with a shiver. Hopefully it wouldn't be long before they could start again, but it was proving tricky. Mary was getting too close for comfort. If she messed up their plans they would have to deal with her first. They wanted to avoid that if at all possible. Murder wasn't part of the long term prospects.

The expected phone call was made. "Yes she's fine. Asleep again. Those sleeping tablets you gave me really knock her out."

"Good but I think it would be good if we bring our plans forward sooner than expected. There is too much sniffing around for my liking. We don't want anyone suspecting anything untoward."

"Are they getting close?"

"I'm not sure but I don't think we can risk it. Questions are being asked. I think they have been put off but you never know. They haven't spoken to me yet."

"That's something positive I suppose."

"You don't sound so sure."

"That's because I'm not."

The call was abruptly disconnected. This was how they usually did it, no goodbyes or anything. Usually the calls were very brief but this one had gone on a bit longer than was safe. They just wanted to be ultra cautious and not risk being overheard or the police turning the spotlight on to them.

They were sure they were doing the right thing, not just for themselves but for Beth as well. Beth's life with her mother couldn't be the best and as for her father well.....

Chapter Thirteen

Carol and Adam rushed to the river, hurrying over to CID who had arrived and taken control of the situation a short while before the two officers.

"Who is it?" asked Carol fearfully. She didn't relish having to ask Mary to identify the body.

"It's an adult male, naked."

"Is it related to our case?"

"We don't know. It could just be a stag do gone wrong."

"But if that were the case he would presumably have been reported missing or an ambulance called if his mates saw the incident."

"They may have all been so drunk they didn't realise how serious it was."

"I don't buy that," said Carol.

"Neither do we, but we have to cover all angles until we can identify the body and then we'll know what we are dealing with."

"Do you want us to see the body? We might have an idea of who it is."

"What do you think?" asked Adam of Carol. "If we were taking bets I'd say it's Jez. He is the only known missing person right now."

"We don't know he's missing, though do we."

"Not for sure no. We do however know we can't find him and we've had so many other officers looking for him up and down the country."

"What about Anne Marie? She was with him."

"Do we know that for certain? We're making an awful lot of assumptions here aren't we?"

The two officers stopped their petty squabbling and followed the sergeant over to the crime scene. The body was now out of the water and on a sheet awaiting further examination to be carried out by forensics when they turned up.

Carol and Adam glanced down at the body. Carol gasped and swayed. She would have fallen if she hadn't have been grabbed by Adam.

"Hey are you all right? I thought you were going to pass out on me then."

"It's just that I know him. It looks like Mr Stubbs."

Adam took a closer look and sure enough he recognised the teacher as well.

"Well that's a nice mess for us to investigate if you're sure," said the DS.

"We are," said Adam for Carol had moved a few steps away as terrible nausea had overcome her. She didn't want to vomit over the crime scene and contaminate any evidence.

"I think you had better question Mary and Maddy again. They are the top of the list in my book. Both have a strong motive."

"It wouldn't be Mary she's too busy grieving for her lost daughter. Her mind is focused on getting her back."

"But she knew about Mr Stubbs and his involvement with the girls. She could easily have approached him believing he knew what had happened to the child. One thing could have led to another and she killed him."

Carol nodded and she and Adam turned to walk back to the car.

"I'm not looking forward to this," said Carol.

"Neither am I," said Adam. "I'll take the lead if you like."

Carol nodded and turned the key in the ignition and off they went. It was at a very slow pace, being stuck at roadworks and it was rush hour. The roads were typically chaotic.

Ten minutes later they turned up at Mary's.

When sitting on the sofa they both turned to her, Adam speaking first as agreed. "We want to know if you have seen Mr Stubbs recently?"

Mary pursed her lips in thought and shook her head. "Why would I? I didn't go to parents evening this time. It didn't seem worth it with Beth missing."

"Do you ever see him socially? For instance do you see him drinking in the pub."

"I don't drink and never visit him in the pub or anywhere. To me he's just another teacher involved with my daughter."

"You're daughter is missing. Maybe you think it was him and you wanted to lash out as he has done to you."

Mary shook her head, started to become distressed. "I wouldn't! I wouldn't!"

"It's ok we believe you," said Carol soothing her with her quiet, calming voice.

"Where was he found?" asked Mary.

"We can't disclose that right now," said Carol.

"That poor man."

"Is it? Don't forget we believe him to be a paedophile who likes young girls and has been known to abuse them at school."

. . . .

"You know I was convinced Mary wasn't involved," said Carol.

"I know but we have to cover all bases, you know that. Maybe you're getting too involved here, too protective."

"I'm only doing my job. Maybe I do get involved but it's how I do it. It's what makes me good at it."

"Look I'm not trying to start an argument. Let's get a move on and try and see Mrs Merriweather. Maddy's mum."

Carol nodded in agreement. They made small talk on the way, over the next ten minutes.

Mrs Merriweather opened the door straight away. Her face paled as she heard the news. "Of course I know nothing. I'm not some vigilante you know."

"We believe you but we had to ask. We believe his death to be foul play and you have a motive."

"I see your point but I am no murderer. He's a big guy and don't think I could succeed. He would be strong enough to overpower me."

"That's ok. We were just doing our job. We'll leave you in peace now."

Carol and Adam left feeling suitably chastened.

"Well that told us. What do you think?"

"She seemed plausible but somehow I'm not convinced," replied Carol.

"She's an angry woman with a child to defend. Most mothers would die for their children. If their children are at risk they will do what it takes."

"Maybe we should speak to her again."

"When we have a bit more to go on would be better. At the moment we know nothing."

Adam agreed and Carol drove back to the crime scene to see what else was happening.

"How did you get on?" asked DS Macintosh.

"Both women flat out denied all knowledge."

"Did you believe them?"

"I believed Mary but Mrs Merriweather was a bit cagey in her denial. I think she might warrant further questioning when we have something else to go on. We can't ask for an alibi or anything because we don't have any timescale to go by."

"I can help you out there. The doctor thinks it could be between midnight and one a couple of days ago."

"I think that would rule out Mrs Merriweather as she would never leave her daughter like that in the middle of the night."

"You sure about that. Just now you thought she would do anything to defend Maddy."

"I know but this is the middle of the night we are talking about. That's a whole different ball game. I'm not saying we shouldn't question her but we should follow other avenues of investigation first."

The DS nodded. "What about you Adam? What do you think?"

"I agree with Carol on this one. I trust her instincts. She is usually right. We should consider Jez as a suspect. We know he can be violent, look what he did to a poor defenceless elderly lady."

"Jez is missing still though, with no sightings."

"I know but we know he must be somewhere around for him to beat the elderly lady up as he did."

The DS nodded. "I'm inclined to agree with you. What you've said makes sense."

"I think it might be worth paying another visit to his neighbour and see if he has been back at all. She's a wonderful source of information."

"That's if she's willing to talk to us. She may be too scared after the last time. I also think we should be wary so as not to cause further trouble for her," said Carol.

"What strikes me as odd is how he knows what is going on when he hasn't even been home. It suggests to me he may have someone keeping an eye out or he's staying with someone in the area. It might be worth doing a door to door to find out. It might also keep his neighbour safe if we are seen talking to everyone."

"Great when do you want us to start?"

"I'm just going to phone through for more officers to help out. I want you both to concentrate on the neighbour as you have already had dealings with her. She may feel safer talking to both of you."

The two officers nodded and went back to the car ready to interview the neighbour.

"I feel a bit worried about going back there," said Carol.

"I know what you mean but I agree with the DS it needs to be done. There has to be someone who can lead us to Jez in that immediate area. It may be someone unlikely that he has threatened into doing it."

"You don't think it could be his neighbour do you. We don't know what he may have said after he had finished beating her. She would be too frightened to refuse. What if he's even hiding out in her house, believing it to be the safest place now he has her where he wants her," said Adam.

"You are complicating things. I don't think he would have the intelligence to come up with such a theory."

"You could be right. Any way we better get on. We can't sit here all day discussing the situation. It won't get anything done and the DS won't be happy."

"He certainly won't. Oh well let's get to it." He opened the door and climbed out of the car, waiting for Carol to get out.

There was no answer to the doorbell. Carol looked at Adam who said, "We should check round the back. "

Carol nodded, saying, "I agree and It's not normal for her to be out. She doesn't get out much, certainly not since she was assaulted so badly."

"I'm going round the back. You wait here."

"I'm not staying there on my own I'm right with you."

"Coward," said Adam with a grin. He knew that Carol was anything but a coward but he enjoyed teasing her.

They walked through the gate when Carol stopped and gasped. Before her was such beauty that she had never seen. A large garden with flowers and plants of every description and colour laid before her. There was a beautifully manicured garden. It was obvious someone loved their garden very much.

They came across some patio doors which stood open. Carol's face changed to one of concern. "She wouldn't have gone out without closing and locking up. She's too security conscious for that."

"Let's go in."

"Are you sure? Maybe we should call it in first."

"We haven't got time. What if she's lying in their injured."

Adam was the first to step inside the house with Carol close on his heels. They looked around but found nothing unusual. Adam pointed to the stairs and Carol nodded. There was no need for conversation they were so used to each other always being able to understand every indication. Up the stairs they looked in the first door they came to. Empty. The next one was the bathroom which was empty as well. Peering in the only other door Adam gasped and rushed inside. Carol looked and saw the elderly lady laying on the floor with her eyes closed. How long had she been like that? Carol hated to think. Adam was on his phone calling it in and asking for an ambulance. Carol breathed a sigh of relief. An ambulance meant she was alive at least.

"Is she?"

"She's alive but her pulse is very faint. I just hope we've come just in time. There is no indication she has been assaulted again."

"We'll have to wait for the paramedics and hope she comes round to tell us what happened. We need to know what we are dealing with."

"Do you think it's foul play?" asked Carol.

Adam shrugged. "I don't know. Only she can tell us that. Everything is immaculate so it's impossible to tell. There is certainly no sign of disturbance. There are no obvious sign of wounds on her at least not fresh ones."

Sirens could be heard getting closer. The two officers breathed sighs of relief that help was here at last. It had seemed so long but was actually only a few minutes since Adam had put the call through.

Suddenly there was a flurry of activity as paramedics rushed in. Adam moved out of the way so they could work.

"What's happened here?" one of them asked.

"We don't know," said Adam taking the lead. "This is what we found when we arrived."

"Pulse faint," said one of the paramedics. "We need to get her to the ambulance."

"Is she going to be all right?" asked Carol.

"Impossible to tell until we do some checks and get her to hospital."

"I'll come with you," said Carol. "In case she should wake up."

"In my opinion she is unlikely to wake up before we get her to hospital. She is completely unresponsive and with that faint pulse she needs a doctor."

"I'd still like to come."

Adam spoke, "I'll follow behind in the car."

Carol climbed in the ambulance after the elderly lady was taken in on a trolley. The journey to hospital was uneventful. She did not regain consciousness but was stable according to the paramedic who was keeping an eye on her vital signs.

Arriving at the hospital she was rushed into the resuscitation room immediately. The paramedics having called it in so staff were ready to receive her. Carol was not allowed in at this point so she waited outside the door, eager for any news. The staff had assured her they would let her know if there were any change but were not hopeful that Carol would be able to speak to her. The nurse, although not saying it aloud, thought it unlikely she would regain consciousness. She was gravely ill.

Adam rushed in about ten minutes later. "How is she?"

Carol shrugged, "I don't know. They rushed her straight into resus and no one has gone in or out since."

"It's serious then."

Carol nodded. "The impression I got in the ambulance is that they don't expect her to survive."

"We'll never know what happened then. We won't be able to get Jez for that."

"You think this is down to Jez?"

Adam nodded.

"But why would he need to do this to her, he's already threatened and beaten her up. Isn't that enough?"

"Maybe she knows more than she's telling or he thinks she does."

Carol said, "I'm not so sure. There is no sign of a new injury so how could he have done it."

Adam shook his head. "I hadn't thought all the ins and outs of it I just felt because he had a go once he might do it again."

"I suppose it's possible," said Carol doubtfully.

"I think all we can do is hope and pray she regains consciousness enough to tell us what happened or that the doctors find something."

"You said pray, I didn't have you down as the praying type."

"I'm not usually. Just in some situations I think that's all we've got going for us. I was brought up to go to church. My parents are still regular church goers. I never did have a faith and since being in the police I've seen too much that suggests there isn't a God."

Carol nodded, knowing what he meant.

They lapsed into silence each lost in their own thoughts. It was during the silence the doctor emerged. The two officers stood up eagerly.

He shook his head, "I'm sorry, she never regained consciousness. We did our best but it wasn't enough. She'd had a massive heart attack. There was no hope of coming back from that."

Carol looked at Adam with tears in her eyes. She had liked the feisty old lady who was never the sort to give up.

"Maybe if she had been found sooner she would have survived."

The doctor shook his head, "It wouldn't have made any difference. She was in too bad a way."

"Is there any way of telling if the heart attack was caused by anything sinister."

"Unlikely. There were no other signs of trauma except the old bruises which you already knew about. No, in my mind no one else was involved."

Carol's face dropped, "Ok thank you for all you did anyway."

Carol and Adam left the hospital in silence. Carol's face was full of disappointment even though she had known deep down that this was going to happen.

"Back to the station?" asked Adam, as he started the car.

"I don't know. Should we go back and help with the search."

"I think we need to go back to the station and report this. It's up to the sergeant what he wants us to do from there."

"I see your point. I just need to be doing something."

"I know how you feel. I'll phone it through and see what they want us to do next. That way we're not wasting precious time."

Carol nodded and sat quietly while Adam made the call.

The call over Adam turned and looked at Carol. She looked at him expectantly.

"We're to go and see how the search is going before going back and writing up the notes."

"Great, that at least makes me feel more useful."

Adam, following his orders, made his way back to the small cul de sac where the old lady had lived next door to Jez and Anne Marie.

"You're back then," commented Jeremy, another officer.

Adam nodded, "She died of a massive heart attack. Apparently there was no hope of survival although they tried everything."

"I'm sorry," said Jeremy turning to Carol whose face showed how she felt.

"We've done all the houses this side it's just the other side and the houses down there at the end."

"Ok we'll take the houses down there," said Adam pointing to the end of the cul de sac.

They walked down the end in silence. Carol still not feeling like talking. In her mind she was still blaming Jez for the death.

Adam knocked on a door which was answered by a young lady with a baby in her arms. "Yes," she queried.

"We are trying to find Jez and Anne Marie whom you may know. They live down there," said Adam pointing in the direction of the house.

"Come in, if you can excuse the mess. I've got my hands full as you can see."

"It's ok no problem," said Carol stepping in first.

"Can you tell us anything you can think of about the couple in question. We need to find them as a matter of urgency."

"Have you tried their house?"

"Yes but there's never anyone in."

"That's strange as I saw Anne Marie come out of there this morning."

Carol and Adam looked at each other. Had the couple been in front of their noses after all.

"I'm a good friend of Anne Marie. I haven't seen too much of her since she got involved with that Jez. I warned her he was a wrongun straight away. He just had that look about him. Sorry I can't put my finger on it, there was something not quite right about him. She wouldn't listen so pretty much dumped me. I think Jez forced her to stop being friends with anyone as I haven't noticed anyone else round there since they got together."

"Have they been there all along or have they been away do you know?" asked Adam when he could get a word in. This lady was quite a talker which was good for them. It could be difficult interviewing people sometimes as they could be shy around the police, worried they would say the wrong thing. In this case all they had to do was listen.

"No they have been there every evening. I watched Jez go into his neighbour the other day. There was a lot of noise but I didn't dare get involved. Jez is a nasty piece of work. If you didn't do as he said you would be beaten to a pulp."

"Do you know why they haven't opened the door to us when he has been there."

"I think they watch out the window quite a lot, or at least Anne Marie does. There is always a curtain twitching. It's possible he makes her do it so he knows when to open the door or not. They probably saw you turn up and that was that. I'm just guessing of course. They could genuinely be out at those times, I have no idea. As I said things have cooled between the two of us so I don't know her every move like I used to."

"Do you think he hurts her?" asked Carol.

"What? No I doubt it. I've never seen a bruise on her. She wouldn't stay with someone like that."

"How do you know? As you said yourself you've lost contact with Anne Marie so how would you know. She could have changed and if she is as in love as you think then it's possible she would forgive him one hundred times over and make excuses for him."

"I suppose," said Eileen.

"Do you mind if we have a look around just to make sure everything's ok?"

"I suppose so. Try not to wake my husband though as he's asleep, he's working nights."

Carol nodded and they stood up. They did a quick tour and ended back in the kitchen. Nothing had been found as had been suggested but they'd had to check anyway, just to satisfy the sergeant and themselves for that matter.

"Ok we'll be off now," said Adam.

"Please call if you think of anything else. You've been most helpful."

Eileen positively blushed which Carol noticed.

"She has a thing for you," said Carol.

"No she didn't you're just being silly now. She had a husband."

"So? When has that stopped a woman from noticing and fancying someone else."

It was Adam's turn to blush.

"Aww, blushing like a schoolboy how sweet," said Carol who couldn't resist teasing him.

"Get away with you," said Adam mortified.

Carol just laughed. She was having some fun here even though Adam wasn't.

"It's all right I'm just winding you up. You're too easy a target."

Adam didn't laugh. He wasn't finding it amusing. Truth be told he was mortified by Carol's teasing.

"Did you find anything out?" asked Jeremy who seemed to be taking the lead in the search.

"Not anything concrete. She was a close friend of Anne Marie's but hadn't had contact since she got together with Jez.

She did say however, that they haven't been away they've been there all along."

"Hmm, that's interesting. Someone else who lives opposite them said much the same thing. He pointed out that everyone is quite scared of Jez. He sounds a bit of a brute really."

"Where do we go from here?" asked Carol, eager to get on.

"You two can head back to the station and report where we're at so far and find out if we should approach his house," said Jeremy, much to Carol's disgust. She liked to be in on the action.

Adam and a thoroughly disgruntled Carol got in the car and set off for the station.

"I don't see why it has to be us. We're missing out on all the action."

"I know but we are the ones that have up to date information. No one else would be able to report back."

"We could tell them."

"Use your brain would that really work? Chinese whispers springs to mind."

"I see your point I suppose," said Carol. She was very reluctant to agree with Adam but it did make sense.

....

They quickly found Sergeant Macintosh and relayed all that had taken place. He put a call into Jeremy and gave permission for them to enter Anne Marie's house. If found they were both to be taken in as it was believed that Anne Marie must know what was going on.

Adam and Carol were to stay where they were as they would be required to conduct the interviews if the couple were picked up.

They sat quietly looking through everything they had to remind themselves before speaking to the wanted pair. Carol was still put out at not being in on the action but she admitted it was better this way.

"We're on," said the sergeant rushing up to them.

"Great," cried an enthusiastic Adam.

"Is it both of them?" asked Carol.

The sergeant nodded in affirmation.

"I suggest we leave them in separate interview rooms for a while to leave them time to think."

Adam and Carol nodded. This was a popular practice in cases like these. They wouldn't know what they had been taken in for. The idea was to take them by surprise. It usually worked and they were hopeful it would in this case as well. They didn't know how much Anne Marie would know but she must be complicit to have kept Jez in her life as she had.

Adam and Carol looked at them through the glass which was one way only. Anne Marie was certainly getting agitated although Jez seemed very calm as if he had nothing to worry about. It concerned Adam and Carol as it could mean a no comment interview. They just hoped that Anne Marie would open up about what she knew.

Carol yawned. She was active by nature and hated all this sitting around waiting. For this reason she knew CID would never be for her. Adam on the other hand was hopeful of moving to them at some point in the near future. He had been told he needed to get more experience on the ground first. He had spent the occasional day with them if they were short staffed or because he was involved in a case they had taken over. He had loved those opportunities and knew it was for him. He had got good feedback as well which encouraged him.

At last they were given the go ahead to begin the interviews, starting with Anne Marie. Doing it this way gave the hope that she would be the more open of the two and might give something away that they could use as leverage with Jez.

"Hello Anne Marie," said Carol. "I assume you know what this is about."

Anne Marie shook her head completely mystified.

Adam and Carol glanced at each other. Maybe it wouldn't be as simple as they had at first thought.

"Ok, well let's start with your neighbour."

"Which one?"

"Come on you must know what we are talking about," said Adam, fully in the bad cop routine.

Anne Marie shook her head innocently. It was difficult for Adam and Carol to be sure if she were genuine or not.

"She died," said a blunt Carol. She was unable to hold it in anymore.

Anne Marie paled slightly but quickly recovered. "I'm sorry to hear that. She was a nice old stick. Very friendly, though a bit nosey."

"So you do know who she is then. Has your memory come back to you now?" asked Adam a touch sarcastically.

"What happened to her?" asked Anne Marie.

"Heart attack," said Carol briefly.

A look flashed across Anne Marie's face. Adam and Carol thought it could have been relief but couldn't be sure.

"You look relieved," said Adam.

Anne Marie shrugged.

"What reason could you have to feel relieved when you heard it was a heart attack.?"

"That it was quick and she didn't suffer."

"How do you know that? You weren't there."

"Well….er… isn't it always like that?"

"Unlikely. She must have been in great pain before the end came. She was alone and must have felt very frightened, unable to get help."

"I'm sorry."

"Why should you be sorry. Come on be straight with us. What do you know?"

"I can't. He'll kill me just like….."

"Just like what?"

Anne Marie hung her head and mumbled something the two officers couldn't quite catch.

"What was that you said?" asked Adam, who was taking the lead now. "Speak up for the tape. We said at the beginning of the interview that it was being recorded."

"Like he did her."

"Who?"

"My neighbour."

"What did he do?"

"He beat her up so badly and he made me watch. Said the same would happen to me if I ever stepped out of line and told anyone."

"She didn't have new bruises on her from the first attack."

"But I assumed it was from him beating her up that caused the eventual heart attack."

"The doctor thinks the two are unconnected."

"It could have been delayed fright."

Adam shook his head. He still felt there was something Anne Marie was not telling them but was unsure what.

"You said just now that you assumed it had been a quick merciful death."

Anne Marie nodded but said nothing.

"It gives me the impression you know more than you're letting on."

Anne Marie's eyes glistened with unshed tears.

"Come on now, you'll feel better if you tell us," said Carol gently.

"I went in there. I used to check up on her before Jez came on the scene. That pretty much stopped when Jez moved in. He didn't approve but I used to go when Jez was out. She had no family you see. No one to look out for her. She was just a lonely old woman that didn't deserve what she got."

"So how was she when you went round?" asked Carol, still in that gentle voice.

"She was ok to start with. Pleased to see me. Suddenly she clutched her chest and collapsed on to the floor."

"Where was this?"

"In the living room."

Adam and Carol looked at each other. This was a load of rubbish. They had found her in the bedroom and in that state wouldn't have been able to move from living room to bedroom.

"What did you do?"

"I checked and she was dead so I left through the patio doors."

"Why didn't you call an ambulance?"

"No point she was dead. There was nothing they could have done."

"But wouldn't it have been the right thing to do instead of leaving her for goodness knows how long to be discovered by someone else."

Anne Marie hung her head and said nothing.

"I don't think you are telling us the truth here."

No response.

"You've admitted to going in so you might as well tell us the truth or we may have to charge you with murder."

"What? I didn't kill her," said Anne Marie, panic in her voice.

"So tell us the truth then."

"Jez went round there again. I tried to stop him but he wouldn't listen he was in a rage and wanted to take it out on someone."

"What was causing him to feel like that."

"Someone had double crossed him or some such nonsense. I don't really know. He didn't let me know what he was up to half the time."

"So he went round there. Then what?"

"He came back pale faced saying she was dead. I wanted to go around to check on her but he said no. He said he'd deal with the body when it got dark and no one would see him."

"Is that what happened next."

"I thought so as he did go out when darkness fell."

"When did you realise he hadn't."

"Just now when you said you'd found her."

"Thank you. But you should have told the truth in the first place. It would have helped. We knew you were lying."

"How?"

"We're not at liberty to disclose that. We can tell you she was alive when we found her."

Anne Marie paled and leaned her head in her hands on the table.

"Are you all right?" asked Carol.

Anne Marie nodded slightly. "So if I had really gone in I would have been able to get help for her."

"Yes," said Carol bluntly.

"Would it have kept her alive?"

Carol shrugged. "Who knows. What we do know is you could have murder on your conscience."

"Will I go to prison?" asked Anne Marie, fear on her face.

"It depends what the CPS say and what else you know or have been involved in."

"You mean there's more?" asked Anne Marie.

"Oh yes there's plenty more, including Jez's missing daughter, we've yet to sort out."

"I don't know about anything else. Of course I knew about his daughter. Everyone does. It's been in the local news."

"Can you look through these photos and see if any of them seem familiar to you."

Adam passed the photos to her and the officers watched her face intently for any sign of recognition. Her face remained blank, until she reached the end then she gasped.

"What is it?" asked Carol.

"My niece Beverley."

"How old is she?"

"Eight. What happened? She looks shocked in this photo as if something has happened."

"We are going to need the address as we need to speak to her and her parents urgently."

"What is it?"

"Sorry we can't tell you any further at this stage. How often do you see them? Have you noticed a difference in Beverley's behaviour."

Anne Marie thought for a while then spoke, "She's been much quieter and clingy towards her mother. She stays away from her father but I don't know why. She screams if she sees Jez so we don't see much of them anymore. Jez doesn't like me going out on my own."

Carol looked at Adam whose face remained expressionless.

"Ok if you can write the address down for me that would be great."

Standing up to leave the room Carol spoke, "Try not to worry too much. We'll be back as soon as we can."

Anne Marie nodded but knew she would worry. Something was definitely going on that they knew about and it seemed to involve her Jez. She knew he was a bit rough and ready, handy with his fists but he had never hurt her. She saw a gentle side of him. He wanted to look after her. He knew if something was wrong and would react accordingly. He was a good bloke really. If he went to prison she would definitely stay with him. Supporting him. She loved him with all her heart. Much better than the scumbag she had been with before.

Chapter Fourteen

"Hello, sorry to trouble you Mrs……"

"Wetherby. Claire Wetherby."

"Claire, we need a chat with you and your daughter Bev."

"Come in," said Claire.

They were led through to a spacious living room where Bev was sat curled up with her head in a book.

"Bev, this is the police. They want to speak to us."

Bev looked at the two officers with a wary look on her face. She could guess what it was about. She hadn't said anything though. He had threatened her if she were to tell. She didn't want anything to happen to her mother or her father.

Carol sat down and looked intently at Bev. A serious girl she decided. Happy with her head in a book.

"What's that you're reading?"

"The Famous Five," said Bev shyly.

"Enid Blyton. I was brought up on her books. They are good aren't they?"

Bev nodded eagerly. It was clear she was an avid reader.

"Now Bev, we have some questions we need to ask you if that's all right."

Bev looked at her mum before nodding. She put her thumb in her mouth, something she still did to comfort herself. She was sure she knew what this was about and didn't want to say anything.

"Did you know Mr Stubbs?"

Claire butted in, "He was their art teacher. Bev asked to be withdrawn from the class very suddenly during the last half of the term. I don't know what happened. Bev started having nightmares and didn't want me to leave her on her own, both in school and out of it."

"What made her insist on leaving art?"

Claire bowed her head. "I don't know. It was about the same time as we moved, but I don't think it was the move."

"Do you want to tell me what happened?" asked Carol sitting beside Bev.

Bev nodded but not enthusiastically. She looked at her mum before speaking as if to get permission. Her mum nodded, trying to be encouraging but very worried at what Bev might come out with. If anyone had hurt her little girl she'd murder them with her bare hands.

Bev was finding it difficult now it came to it. She thought briefly then spoke. "It was at the end of term, just before Christmas. Mr Stubbs had us all helping take down our art work that he said would be kept in the cupboard until next term. When everyone else left he called me back and asked me to help him."

Adam and Carol looked at each other. This was becoming a familiar ritual now. They just hoped that mother and daughter had a firm alibi for when Mr Stubbs was killed whichever method it was.

"He started to touch me and put his hand up my skirt. He suggested I took my jumper off."

"Ok thank you Bev. Do you know the whereabouts of Mr Stubbs now."

"No," she said shaking her head.

"Do you know of anyone else this has happened to?" asked Carol.

Bev shook her head.

"Did you tell anyone?"

Again Bev shook her head. "He said if I did I wouldn't see mummy and daddy again."

Adam and Carol looked at each other. Adam seeing the anger build up inside Carol and her eyes bright with unshed tears. She had been in the job long enough to become hardened to it but was still very sensitive especially where children were concerned. Adam wasn't sure if it was a good thing or bad. It did mean she was a good liaison officer as she could empathise with the victims of this sort of crime.

Claire burst into tears at hearing what Bev had to say. Carol reached out to take her hand but Claire snapped it back.

When the crying had died down a bit she spoke. "How come he was allowed to work with children, young children at that? Don't you have a list for these sorts of people."

Carol said, "Yes we do but he wasn't on it. Somehow he slipped under the radar and no one spoke up until now."

"So there are others?"

"Yes," said Carol. "But it's only just coming to light the extent of his crimes."

"Are we in any danger from him. I wouldn't like to think of Bev disappearing like that other little girl."

"We don't know as yet if there is any correlation between Mr Stubbs abuse and the disappearance of Bethany."

Carol looked at Adam asking with her eyes if she should tell them about the death of Mr Stubbs.

Adam gave a surreptitious shake of his head. It wasn't appropriate at present as the case was still being investigated.

It was a short while later after a period of silence that Adam and Carol made their escape.

"Phew that was intense," said Carol.

"I thought you were going to burst into tears at one point."

"So did I. Fortunately I'm learning not to wear my heart on my sleeve. How they lure the children in is so simple just ask them to go to the store cupboard and that's it they are trapped until the abuser lets them go. Then threaten them with the consequences if they do tell."

"Do you think this could be what happened to Bethany?"

"I don't know since Mary seemed genuinely shocked. Jez is involved in some way so telling him is a waste of time. Maybe she was kidnapped as a warning to the other girls if they were to tell."

"You could be right," said Adam. "But I'm not convinced. I think we're dealing with two separate cases here. I think it's just coincidence with the paedophile case. It's good for the kidnapper as we are put completely off the scent and are just chasing our tails as it were."

"You're probably right."

She was absolutely certain Mary had to be involved with the kidnap somehow because of the lack of breaking in and also someone had a key and that was very few. "I'm not sure I can believe that she didn't know anything about who or why it could have happened."

"Do you think it possible that she was involved with taking her little girl?"

"I'm not sure about that. But we do have to investigate the possibility especially as someone knew exactly what they were doing and where to find Bethany."

"Are you going to see Mary again?" asked Adam. Carol nodded but stayed quiet.

"I'm stuck as to how to proceed with her though. I don't want to put her on her guard and make her suspicious of me but I need to say something. If we look at what we've got, we have a child who goes missing in the middle of the night. No signs of a break in. No ransom note. No genuine contact except this rather dubious message about speaking to Liz. Very few people have a key to the house."

"Hmm it's a difficult one. I can see your dilemma. On the surface it does look bad for Mary. The question it poses for me though is how distraught she is. Would she be that distraught if she were involved in some way however small?"

"You've got a point she has seemed on the edge of a precipice."

"Exactly."

"It's so hard," said Carol. "I think this is the most difficult case I've come across in my experience of being family liaison."

"Are you getting too involved with Mary that you can't see clearly?"

"No it's not that, it's just…oh I don't know."

"Look, instead of dropping you off at Mary's why don't I carry on to the station. You never know maybe you'll find inspiration or advice on the way forward."

"Good idea. At least it's an excuse to avoid seeing Mary. My other concern is that she may have something to do with Mr Stubbs death. If she wanted to avenge herself of his abuse of Bethany she might do something completely out of character. There must be nothing worse than thinking your child, especially one as young as Bethany, is being abused."

"It's a very difficult, complicated case," said Adam, having nothing more to add on the subject.

"I wish I knew what the answer was and where Bethany is dead or alive."

"I know. I think we need to do a lot more digging. Who knows what other murky secrets are laying dormant, hidden from view."

"You've hit the nail on the head there."

……..

Back at the station they gave their report. Carol took advantage of the time to get some clue as to the way forward with Mary.

Sergeant Macintosh said, "I think the best thing to do is go back to Mary, don't say anything to her about Mr Stubbs, as if she is guilty she might give herself away. The same applies to Bethany's disappearance. We need to see how involved she is or isn't."

Chapter Fifteen

At Mary's house Carol was making herself comfortable, or as comfortable as she could on the overstuffed sofa with the awful lumpy cushions behind her back. She didn't want to appear rude by asking for another chair. Anyway as she could be there for sometime she didn't want to sit on a hard, upright dining chair that would be awful. She would end up feeling terribly bruised.

"How're things going?" Carol asked.

Mary shrugged. "I keep wondering what would have happened if I had stayed on the phone that night whether I would have my Beth back by now."

"You can't know that. Don't beat yourself up about it. It may have just been the perpetrator playing games with you."

"Really?"

"Yes," said Carol, trying to be reassuring. She didn't want to frighten Mary with statistics, but the chances of getting her daughter back through that phone call were nil. As time went on it was becoming more unlikely but again telling Mary that might tip her over the edge. Kidnappers rarely gave their victims back to the family. It wouldn't be safe for them as they could be identified.

"Do you remember us talking about Mr Stubbs?"

Mary nodded before speaking, "That vile man who interferes with young children. It's sick. If I could get my hands on him….."

"You sound angry," said Carol.

"Wouldn't you be if it was your child?"

"Probably," admitted Carol. "Have you made any effort to contact him or gone to the school to catch a glimpse of him?"

Mary was startled, "No why would I? I might do something I'd regret later. I want him punished by the court and to see him rot in jail for the rest of his miserable life."

"That won't happen unfortunately," said Carol.

"Oh why? Surely you've got evidence to charge him."

"Someone got to him first and dealt with him."

"No!" cried Mary. "I hope he's badly hurt. Whoever did this to him I applaud them."

Carol deeply suspicious of the way Mary was talking thought she should be careful what she said to avoid putting words into Mary's head if Mary was in fact the killer.

"You're being very quiet suddenly. What is it you're not telling me?"

"Mr Stubbs is dead," Carol saw nothing of it but to come straight out with it.

"Mary paled, "Dead? What happened? Who?"

"I can't go into more details at the moment," said Carol, not wanting to say more in case they needed to take Mary in to officially question her about the death. She was the number one suspect in Carol's mind.

....

Carol quickly answered the phone when it rang especially when she saw it was Adam.

"I've got to take this outside," said Carol to Mary, excusing herself. "Ok I'm free to speak now."

"Well we've discovered he was killed at approximately nine last night."

"That's specific," said Carol surprised. They were usually unable to give concrete information in situations like this.

"Yeah, his watch was shattered and…"

"Let me guess, it stopped at that time."

"Of course. It wasn't that difficult to guess though so don't start getting big headed about it."

"I'll try not to. Listen I've just been talking with Mary about Mr Stubbs." Carol recounted the conversation she'd had before her phone rang.

"Hmm," said Adam. "Just a minute I'll see what the serge says…..Ok Carol I'm coming to pick you up. He thinks we should formally question Mary."

Carol sighed, "That's what I thought would happen. I feel like a traitor now. I'm supposed to be supporting Mary not arresting her."

"Don't worry you won't be involved with questioning her. Serge said he and I would do that. You can watch through the window."

"That's a relief but I still feel like I'm betraying her in some way."

"This isn't the first time you've had to arrest someone you were acting as liaison officer for."

"I know but that always came after intensive investigation and led to suspicion that it was an inside job if you know what I mean. Whereas this seems a completely separate incident altogether."

"But is it? He could still have taken Beth himself."

"If he did we'll never find out what he did with her. That's a reason why she wouldn't have killed him. She wanted her Beth back."

"Confronting him was unlikely to produce results though."

"Look instead of talking on the phone I must be on my way to you."

"Ok I better go and prepare Mary for the backstabbing."

"You don't have to say anything I could just turn up and take it from there. She need never know you knew about it."

"She's not stupid of course she would guess. I have just been asking her questions then she gets taken to the station to answer more along the same lines."

"I get your point."

They said goodbye and Carol went inside with a heavy heart.

"Mary I'm afraid Adam is on his way. They want to ask you some questions at the station."

"Is it Beth? Have they found her?"

Carol shook her head. How she hated having to see the look of disappointment on her face. "No, I'm afraid not. It's about Mr Stubbs."

"But I've already told you I don't know anything."

"Sorry there's nothing I can do about it. CID are involved and they are above us. We follow their orders."

Mary nodded in understanding but it didn't help Carol who still felt awful for betraying Mary in this way.

It wasn't long before Adam drew up outside. He rang the bell.

"Come on Mary," said Carol holding out her hand.

Mary refused to take the offer of help. She felt as if Carol was swapping sides in this. Until now she had almost forgotten Carol was with the police as she spent so much time with her. It was like being with a close friend. It seemed now as if Carol was her only friend as she hadn't spoken to Liz since that awful day that Liz seemed to betray her in that public way.

In silence Mary opened the door grabbing her coat as she did so. It was a chilly day, dull and overcast although rain hadn't come as yet. It seemed suitable to Mary that she was being taken on such a miserable day after all the lovely sunny days they had had recently. How she wished she could have taken Beth along by the river to see the swans. Beth was fascinated by birds and would stand watching for hours if given a chance. She could just about imagine the sun shimmering down creating a sliver of brightness on the quiet, calm water.

In the car Adam tried to get away from the strained atmosphere that existed between the two women. His chatter was lost on them though as they sat in their own little world, wishing they could put the clock back and pretend this wasn't happening.

All too soon they arrived at the station and Mary found herself sitting in a dull, dark interview room with just the one light which was also very dim. She found herself facing Adam and someone who called himself a sergeant. She missed Carol and wished she was there by her side. With her there she felt she could face anything. She didn't know of course that Carol was watching and hearing everything through the glass down the side. It seemed to Mary as if it was just a mirror.

The sergeant got right down to the nitty gritty after introductions had been made. "You were recently told that Mr Stubbs the art teacher at your daughter's school had abused her and other girls."

Mary nodded, "Yes," she said.

"How did that make you feel?"

"What a stupid question, how was that supposed to make me feel."

Adam and the Sergeant looked at each other. Signs of anger already that was good, maybe they would be getting to the truth sooner than expected.

"I guess I'd be pretty annoyed."

"Well I'm consumed by anger. It eats away at me every moment of everyday. It's left me wondering if he was the evil man that took my daughter away from me."

"What would you do if you were to see him in the street?"

"I don't know, probably shake him until he told me the truth."

"How would you know if it was the truth or not if he denied all knowledge?"

"It's obvious isn't it? He must be the kidnapper. He was obviously punishing me or her in some way. Maybe she threatened to tell someone what had happened between them."

"Where were you last night?"

"At home, why?"

"Can anyone confirm this?" asked Adam ignoring the question Mary had asked.

"No, of course not. Without my daughter I'm alone and lonely. Liz betrayed me so I haven't even got her company now. Even if we were still friends we wouldn't have been together as she has her own child to put to bed."

"I see. Did you watch anything on telly?"

"No sorry. I was just sat there with curtains closed. I just wanted to shut out the world."

....

Carol behind the glass watching the drama thought how Mary seemed to be digging a hole for herself. It was looking more and more as if Mary could be guilty of killing Mr Stubbs. She hadn't wanted to believe it when talking to Adam but watching this it almost seemed inevitable. Carol felt sad for her. Had she been so convinced that she had sought the man out and tried to get a confession out of him. Killing him when he hadn't provided a satisfactory answer. Had she meant to kill him even? Maybe it was a spur of the moment thing and she was horrified at what she had done.

"What's this all about anyway?"

"Mr Stubbs was found dead today. Have you got anything to add."

Mary shrugged but kept quiet. What was there to say. Dead, how final that sounded. She couldn't pretend to be sad when she wasn't. She was glad. Inside she was dancing. At least he couldn't hurt anymore young girls. She felt her Beth had been avenged.

"Have you nothing to say?" asked Adam when the silence had been going on too long.

"What am I supposed to say? I'm not sorry he died, I can't be after what he did to my Beth."

"You don't seem even a little bit curious as to how he died," commented Adam.

"Why should I be? I want to shake hands with the person who had the guts to do something about it."

Adam and sergeant Macintosh looked at each other, the sergeant giving a slight nod. They stood up and left the room to go and confer with Carol to see what input she had.

"I hate to say this but I think she's guilty," said Carol as soon as they appeared.

"But wouldn't you be glad if the abuser who had hurt your daughter was dead?"

Carol thought for a while before saying, "You've got a point but I still think she's guilty. She hasn't even asked how he died so she doesn't know it's murder but she's making an assumption that it was."

"You're right there," said Adam.

The sergeant stood listening to the two officers chatting. He found that listening to others could often give insight to what was happening, so they could come to the right conclusion.

"Right let's go back in there and see what comes up. I think we need to be a bit firmer with her. More of the bad cop routine."

Back in the room with Mary the questioning began again.

"You don't seem surprised he's dead and you seem to assume someone was responsible. That's a big assumption to make."

"I….I….I…" Mary stuttered, realising too late that she wasn't helping herself.

"It's obvious isn't it? He was a young man so is unlikely to have died of natural causes."

"What about an accident, that hasn't occurred to you either," said the sergeant, entering the conversation for the first time.

"I don't know what to say," said Mary. She was digging herself in too far and she didn't know how to get out of it. All she knew for certain was that she was in deep trouble.

The two officers didn't want to reveal the manner of death in case their number one suspect should let something slip later.

"Right I think it's time to have a rest. We'll resume this interview later. Mary you'll be taken to one of the cells for a while. You need to do some serious thinking."

"But you can't do that. I'm innocent. I haven't done anything wrong."

"No, in your eyes you probably haven't. You were trying to right a terrible wrong."

"I didn't kill him or anyone else. Instead of looking into the death of a paedophile, who is no loss to society, you should be concentrating your efforts into finding out what happened to my daughter. I just want my daughter back."

Adam looked at her with some sympathy. She really did seem lost without her daughter.

"Did she tell you what happened and you were so horrified you needed to purify your daughter whose innocence had been taken away? Maybe that was a step too far as well," said the sergeant.

"But she disappeared in the middle of the night and there was that phone call," pointed out Mary.

"That's what you tell us," he said rather harshly. "It's a bit hard to believe though that such a phone call ever took place. A robotic voice, now don't you think that's a bit too sci fi to be believed."

Mary started to panic. It looked as if they were blaming her for that as well. She hadn't a clue what to do. If this was the way things were going then she'd never find out what happened to her daughter. Tears started to run down her cheeks. It all seemed so hopeless and she didn't know what to do. Liz would know but how could she contact her when they hadn't spoken for a couple of weeks. What help would Liz even be when she thought she should give up on finding her daughter and accept she'd gone for good. Could she risk it, if they even allowed her a phone call.

When requested, she was surprised when they agreed. She was taken to the phone and the officer made the call and when Liz answered passed the phone to Mary.

"Liz I'm so glad you're in. I'm in trouble. I'm at the police station. Mr Stubbs is dead and they seem to think I was involved in some way. They also seem to be blaming me for Bethany going missing. My little girl. What am I going to do. If that's what they think I'll never find out what happened."

"First of all calm down. Take some slow deep breaths….That's right. Now tell me slowly what is happening."

Mary repeated her story this time slower and making more sense.

"I think the best thing I can do would be to find a solicitor for you. They should be able to help you more than I can."

"I won't be able to pay you back though. I don't have that sort of money."

"Don't worry about that. We can sort something out at a later date when all this is over."

"Thank you so much. I really didn't know what to do."

"No problem. I'm happy to help. I've missed you."

"I've missed you too. Friends again?"

"Of course," said Liz.

Mary put the phone down greatly relieved. At least she was going to get help now as she really didn't know what to do.

When Mary's actions were fed back to CID the sergeant breathed out a large sigh. This was what he didn't need, a solicitor. He knew how things would go now. It would be an inevitable no comment interview. Nothing further would be found out.

Liz, true to her word, found a solicitor free at that moment who could go and speak to Mary and advise her.

When Mr Jackson the solicitor saw Mary, he felt pity for her. She was sat in her cell with reddened eyes and puffy cheeks which told of all the weeping she had done. Not surprisingly really. She was having a nightmare of a day that's for sure. Virtually accused of murder and of arranging for her own daughter to disappear. That was too much in anybody's book. Even a habitual criminal would struggle with this scenario.

"Are you ok Mary," he asked gently.

Mary shook her head. She couldn't put up a pretence any longer.

"I think first of all we need to give a no comment interview. Whatever they say you are to respond with that. It's imperative you say no more on the subject. However they may try and goad you into saying more than you should."

Mary nodded her understanding.

It wasn't long before she was taken to an interview room to continue the questioning which was exhausting her. The solicitor accompanying her.

The presence of the solicitor annoyed the police questioning her. They were no longer getting anywhere. After some thought the sergeant decided to take a more drastic approach to shock her into reacting.

He showed her the photo of the dead body after it had been taken out of the water. She gasped. Surely he hadn't drowned as that could just be an accident.

"That could be an accident and he fell in while out for a walk."

"That sounds a bit implausible. Anyway we have the proof that it was murder."

"No, no , no, no," shouted Mary, starting to lose it.

Mr Jackson placed a hand on Mary's arm in a gesture of support and also to try and ground her in the here and now to avoid her saying anything further on the subject.

"If you know it's murder why aren't you out there trying to find a murderer instead of making assumptions about my client."

"I'm only doing my job."

"Is it really necessary to go in so hard. You can see how fragile she really is. Going back to that cell will kill her."

"We have to keep her locked up you know that. She's in the frame for two serious crimes."

Mr Jackson sighed, expecting nothing more. He had met the sergeant on several other cases he had worked on and he was known as a strict disciplinarian. He went at things until he got the result he was seeking. He didn't seem to care whether it was the right result. He supposed it was all about targets these days rather than real work. Find a likely suspect and assume the worst until they confessed just to shut him up more like. He could get people to doubt themselves very easily and Mary was particularly fragile.

"If you were in our position you would see we have no choice. Everything points to Mary."

"Are you sure about that? From what I understand it could just as easily be her ex Jez whom you were showing an interest in."

"He will be questioned in due course."

"When? After you've destroyed and charged my client."

"Evidence all points to her. She was alone at home with her daughter when she went missing. There was no break in. You must see it looks suspicious, especially when she talked of a robotic voice on the phone which sounds completely implausible. She has reason to go after Mr Stubbs after she found out that he was abusing kids at school including her Bethany."

"Jez could easily be the culprit, he could have had access to the house and taken his daughter. He could have killed Mr Stubbs for getting found out and to ensure he didn't say anything about their little activity with young girls."

"He was with his new partner Anne-Marie, unless you're suggesting she was involved as well."

"It's possible."

"You're only saying that to get your client off the hook. I could charge you with obstruction."

"Oh really, this is now getting out of hand. That's going too far even for you."

The sergeant shrugged. He knew he was a hard taskmaster. It got the job done though. It got them the results they needed.

"How long do you expect to keep my client in that cell?"

"As long as it takes. I don't have to justify myself to you."

Mr Jackson sighed and went off back in the direction of the cells to Mary. It had been a pointless argument. He felt stupid for even trying but he had to say something, even though he knew the sergeant too well. This wasn't the first battle they'd had and it probably wasn't the last.

…………

Meanwhile the sergeant asked Adam and Carol to interview Anne-Marie. He had decided to speak to her first as he thought it might give them some leverage to get at Jez.

Preliminaries over with Adam spoke to Anne-Marie, "Those photos we showed you, have you any further thoughts?"

"Like what?"

"Where they had come from would be a good start."

"Dunno," said Anne Marie suddenly turning sulky. This approach she usually found worked if she didn't want to talk about a specific topic. At least it had worked up until now.

"Not good enough. You're not stupid, you must have some idea. Something that seems to involve Jez."

"He wouldn't get involved in anything like that, he's got a young daughter himself. He'd kill anyone who……" she stopped abruptly as she realised what she was saying.

Adam had a triumphant look on his face. She had let too much out and now she couldn't take it back. "Kill, you say, is that what he did to your neighbour because she was telling us about him. Do you know something about Mr Stubbs death maybe?"

Anne Marie stayed silent not wanting to say anything in case she gave herself away again.

"Come on you might as well tell us all you know. You've already said so much, you might as well carry on."

"You know he wasn't interested in his daughter, never had been, so why would he show his concern by killing someone who had abused her," Anne Marie was back pedalling trying to get them out of the hole she had dug.

"Come on you can't get away with that when you started to say something just now. Spit it out, you may as well. I don't think you're the sort of person who has regular contact with the police. You must hate it in here. The quicker you tell us what we need to know the sooner you can leave."

Anne Marie sighed, not knowing what to do. She really didn't want to get Jez into trouble but she wasn't used to this happening. All her other boyfriends had been law abiding citizens. She was unsure what attracted her to Jez who was a wild one that was for sure.

"He was angry when he found out about Mr Stubbs abusing kids including his daughter. He started ranting and raving. It took me by surprise and scared me somewhat. I had never seen this side of Jez before, and I didn't like it."

"Go on," said Carol, speaking for the first time.

"I thought he was going to hit me so I withdrew but he continued. He punched his fist into the wall making a dent in it, he hit it so hard. He said he was going out. Scared at what he might do I followed him. He didn't want me and tried to stop me getting in the car but I insisted. He took off so fast that I thought we would have an accident. I tried to get him to slow down but he wouldn't, told me to stop whinging. We drew up by the park and he got out. He told me to stay in the car but I wouldn't and I followed him. There was a man sitting on the bench next to the pond. Jez roared and put his hand round the man's throat."

"Did you recognise the man?" asked Carol, breaking into the monologue.

Anne Marie shook her head. "I'd never seen him before but Jez knew him. He called him Stubbs so I assume he's the one you were talking about."

"I'm interested in what Jez said to him. We already know he had the collection of photos hidden so he has to be involved in the paedophile ring. Probably the boss."

"Jez said how did you manage to get caught. You knew you had to be careful but you obviously went after the wrong girls."

"It wasn't my fault was it. They would never have found the photos if your daughter hadn't gone missing."

"It wasn't me that took her. I had enough of her when we were together. It was hard trying to stay away from her. I was worried I wouldn't have been able to keep my hands off her."

"Carry on," said Carol for Anne Marie had stopped.

Wiping her eyes she continued. "Sorry it's so hard to relive. My Jez is obviously not the sort of person I thought he was."

"I know it's hard but you need to carry on," said Carol gently.

"I'm scared of what he'll do to me when he realises it's my fault for telling you everything."

"You'll be safe, there are steps we can take."

Anne Marie nodded before continuing, "He pulled the man off the bench and forced him nearer the pond. Suddenly I saw him grab a large branch from a nearby tree that had fallen to the ground. He lifted his hand and swung it hard onto the man's head."

Anne Marie stopped and began to retch. Adam and Carol stayed quiet waiting for it to subside and for Anne Marie to compose herself.

"He fell into the water. I gasped. Jez turned back to me and said if I told anyone it would be me next. I felt so frightened I haven't dared leave his side since in case he thinks I'm telling someone. I'm not like that. I should have listened when friends told me I shouldn't get involved with him, he was trouble."

Tears poured down her cheeks. "I haven't slept properly since. Thinking of that poor man face down in the water. The nightmares are too much but all this doesn't seem to bother Jez who has snored his head off every night."

"Thank you. You've done really well to tell us all of this."

Adam and Carol stood up, ready to leave the room, relieved that at least part of the investigation seemed to be over.

. . . .

The interview with Jez was not going according to plan. To everything they said he responded with "no comment". Adam and Carol were getting very frustrated. They did everything they could to shock him into answering but nothing. They were no further forward thirty minutes later when they stood up with a sigh.

"We'll leave you for a while to think about your position here. We have enough to charge you but would like to hear your version of events," said Adam as the two officers left the interview room.

"Grr! I feel like wringing the man's neck. He is sat there so calmly and looking so innocent and shocked at what he was hearing," said Carol in the luxury of the canteen getting a cup of much needed coffee. She had the feeling it was going to be a long afternoon.

"I know what you mean. I feel he's just mocking us," replied Adam.

"There must be something we can use to get some sort of reaction instead of that blank face and sneering smile."

"I know, but can't think of anything for the moment."

"Hello, what are you too looking so glum about?" asked Jo, another PC and family liaison officer.

"You know this paedophile ring we are working on? Well our prime suspect as leader of the gang and murderer of another member has just given a no comment interview. I want to wipe that smirk off his face. He's certain we have nothing and he'll get away with it if he keeps quiet."

"Well," said Jo, "I might just be able to make your day. Someone has just come in with their young daughter…"

Carol interrupted, "Now let me guess she has been molested as well at school with Mr Stubbs?"

Jo shook her head grinning, "Not exactly but Jez was involved. The child didn't know his name but it definitely wasn't Stubbs who was stood watching it take place. The mother and child have agreed to do an id parade to see if Miranda can identify the man."

"Wow, I don't believe it. Let's hope she can identify Jez then we've got some leverage with him which might lead to him giving himself away."

"You think so," said Carol. "I wouldn't be so sure. As slippery as an eel that one."

....

"Ok Miranda," said Jo kneeling down so she was at the same height as the small child. "You have to go along the row of men. Look carefully at each one and nod or shake your head if you recognise him."

Miranda nodded slowly. She wasn't sure about this but had been reassured that she was doing a good thing here. Her mummy had promised a pizza if she was a good girl and identified the scum. She didn't know what scum meant but her mummy had used it so it must be ok.

Slowly going along the row looking at each man in turn. When she reached number nine she paused longer than the others. Jo held her breath, would she do it? It was nerve wracking watching and waiting for her answer.

Miranda slowly turned to Jo and nodded her head. Jo went up to her and asked again to confirm it was indeed number nine. Jo breathed a small sigh of relief as Miranda nodded her head when looking at Jez. They had him. The small child had done a good job.

Jo had a big smile on her face as she approached Adam and Carol.

"You got him then," said Carol, stating fact.

Jo nodded. "She identified him straight away. More than what I had hoped for. I was worried she was too young to be able to do this accurately. Just goes to show even at that young age they can still recognise people involved in a crime.

Chapter Sixteen

Carol and Adam were feeling on top of the world as they went back to interview Jez. They were even more sure they had him now. Nothing could get him out of this.

"Ok," said Adam. Face impassive as he began talking to Jez. "Well guess what we've been doing since we were last here. We had a nice little chat with another officer which turned out quite nice for us, but not for you maybe."

"You've got nothing on me," sneered Jez.

"Haven't we? How do you account for a man matching your description molested a young seven year old at her school. Mr Stubbs looked on."

"That's below the belt using Mr Stubbs to get at me now he's dead."

"How do you know he's dead?" said Carol butting in.

Adam and Carol didn't dare look at each other. It would have felt too cruel as well, especially as Carol had the desire to laugh welling up inside. She knew she couldn't show any sign of weakness here. Jez would jump on it straight away.

"Didn't you tell me earlier?" asked Jez confidently.

"May have done," said Adam. "Now answer the question."

"He was lying there dead," began Jez. "I tried to stop her I really did but she was all over him, it made me sick. She hit him over the head and said he would rot in hell over this. She was like a woman scorned, and that is not a pleasant sight let me tell you. She laughed as she saw him hit the water. She insisted we get together and come up with a suitable story should we need it. I can't lie anymore, who knows what she's capable of. I could be the next victim. She has anger issues you know."

"This isn't the urgent tales we heard from Anne Marie. Who do you think is telling the truth?"

"Well I know I am so you should look closer to home."

Adam and Carol left the room. They needed a break to think things through and seek the sergeant for further advice. It was turning into his word against hers and with no witnesses to come forward it was going to be hard to charge anyone.

"Ok well I think you need to turn to Anne Marie again. Confront her with what he is saying and see what her response is. You never know it could all be a pack of lies from one of them."

Carol sighed. It should have been so simple but no, it had to turn into a pear shaped farce. A game of he said, she said. How she hated it when cases became like this as they so often did. She preferred it nice and simple. Was it even possible that Jez was innocent? But if so who was guilty? Someone had to have killed Mr Stubbs and Jez or Mary seemed the only obvious suspects.

....

Back with Anne Marie again, Adam and Carol were determined to get at the truth.

"We've spoken to Jez and he denies all knowledge of what you've alleged. He's unable to explain what happened."

Anne Marie stayed silent as Adam and Carol waited patiently for a response they were sure would come. They expected the silence to become uncomfortable and then Anne Marie would speak but it showed no sign of happening.

"Have you got nothing to say?" asked Adam.

"There's nothing to say," said Anne Marie. "I can't help it if Jez denies everything. I can't make him tell the truth."

"I understand that but it makes it difficult for us to decide who is telling us the truth here. Unless you can come up with anything else that is."

"Did you find the branch that he used to hit Mr Stubbs with. It should be blood stained as there were signs of blood in the water when he went in."

"We haven't found that or anything else that could be used as a weapon."

Anne Marie looked surprised at this. "There must be, he didn't take it anywhere he just let go and it fell to the ground. Straight after that he sank on to the bench and seemed to be breathing heavily as if it had taken all his strength. His head went into his hands and he stayed there not moving."

"What did you do?" asked Adam.

"Stayed where I was watching the events. I sensed that Jez didn't want me or anyone else around at the time. He needed to be alone to think about what he had just done and what his next move would be."

"Didn't you consider going up to him and comforting him. After all you're supposed to be his partner."

"I know him well. He wouldn't want me to see him weak like that. He hated any sort of weakness in himself or others."

"Think. Is there anything else you can think of that might help our enquiries. We still need to hear more about Jez and if you have any insight into his and Mary's marriage."

"They hadn't been happy for a long time. At least that's what he told me. He was very upfront about his marriage and impending divorce."

"Ahh the divorce factor. Always dangerous to get involved with someone else's marital drama. It never ends prettily."

"I never have before. It's an unwritten rule I have. Getting involved in someone else's marriage is only going to end badly. Not in this case though. Jez has been really good to me. A true gentleman."

Carol tried to hide a burst of laughter not very successfully, Jez a gentleman was just taking things too far. Admittedly she had become hardened over time but it still seemed so weak still. She was sure Jez would still give a no comment reply as always. He wouldn't even blush just give the answer he felt like giving. He was a pro at it. Must have had lots of practice in the past, although he had no criminal record until now. His luck had finally run out. They had him, she was sure of that.

"Did you know Jez had a child?"

"Yes he told me that soon after I met him. He wanted to be completely upfront about his life so I knew what I was getting into."

Carol looked cynical, "But he never told you about his tendency towards young girls did he?"

Anne Marie shook her head. "He didn't. In fact it was the complete opposite. He made it very clear he didn't want children. Couldn't stand them he said. This was the reason he gave for his marriage breaking down. He didn't want to know Bethany and Mary had refused to have an abortion when he suggested it."

"You didn't question him on this? After all it's a strange way to act over your own child."

"I didn't think anything about it actually. He seemed genuinely upset about it. I felt sad for myself as I wanted children but I accepted his views on this and loved him enough to be with him without them. Brats, he used to call them. It was an awful shock when you showed me the photos. It makes sense now as to why he didn't want to be around children. He obviously didn't want to risk giving himself away."

"Very clever. He must have really hated it when the photos got discovered and the abuse started to be uncovered as well."

"He was furious and insisted it was nothing to do with him. He even insisted that Mary must have had a relationship with Mr Stubbs after they broke up and that's how the photos got there."

Carol asked, "Did you believe him?"

"At first yes. I believed everything he said at that time without question. Not any longer. He had me fooled that's for sure."

Carol and Adam left the room. They weren't sure they had anymore to go on but felt they had all they could get out of Anne

Marie. Now they needed to go back to the slippery worm as they had coined Jez between themselves.

………..

"So Jez tell us again how the photos got into your house if you weren't involved?"

"No comment."

"How long can you keep up this no comment? We know everything now so it's not going to help you get away with anything."

"Like what? I'm innocent of everything."

"What's that exactly?" asked Adam who was again taking the lead.

"Everything you think I've done."

"Unless you tell us we don't know do we."

"No comment."

"You could tell us what you are innocent of or we might charge you for crimes you didn't actually commit."

"I didn't take Beth. I don't know where she is and I don't care either."

Carol and Adam looked at each other. Was he going to give himself away after all.

"I didn't kill Mr Stubbs that was Anne Marie as I've already told you."

"She has a different story."

"She would. It was her idea to kill him but I'm not the violent type so refused to get involved. It frightened me actually to hear and see her anger. I hadn't realised she was like that."

"How did she kill him?"

"She ran at him quite fast with her arms outstretched which pushed him in the water. I think he hit his head on something as he became very still face down in the water."

"And you didn't try and help him?"

Jez shook his head. "I was scared if I did I'd meet the same fate as he did."

"Anne Marie tells a completely different story."

"She would, wouldn't she. She needs to hide her own guilt."

"What reason did she have to kill Mr Stubbs?"

"To protect me of course. She didn't want him to have a chance to tell you lot anything."

"About what?"

"The photos of course."

"Why would that be protecting you if you knew nothing about them and weren't involved."

Jez fell silent, maybe realising he'd given himself away.

"Lost your tongue?" asked Adam, trying to hide a smile.

"No comment."

"I suggest Anne Marie was telling the truth and you are up to your eyes in trouble now."

"No comment."

"You can say that as much as you like but you've already said enough. I don't think we need to continue. We will confer with our boss but are sure we have enough to charge you with everything."

"I didn't take Beth. You have to believe me. I didn't even want her. I tried to persuade Mary to have an abortion. Charge me with everything else if you want but not that."

The two officers left the room jubilantly. They'd got what they'd wanted to get.

"Well done, you two," the sergeant congratulated them on their success.

"We're still no further forward finding out who took Bethany and where she might be - dead or alive."

"At least we have Jez. The paedophile ring has almost been closed down. We just have to find out who else is involved."

"What about Mary?" asked Carol.

"We let her go for now. We have nothing on her. We need more evidence about Beth's disappearance before looking at her again."

Carol nodded. "I'm not sure I'll be able to continue to be her liaison officer. She may not trust me anymore."

"We'll take it as it comes. She may prefer to stick to you because she knows you. I hope you can get passed this."

Carol agreed. "What should we do now?"

"Go and release her then give her a lift home. Stay with her awhile and just listen to whatever she wants to say. You may pick up on something just by listening to random chatter."

Chapter Seventeen

Mary and Carol were sat in an uncomfortable silence. Neither happy in each other's presence. Mary felt betrayed and Carol felt guilty. It had been like this since arriving back at Mary's. Adam had kept up a one way conversation in the car but now it was just the two of them.

"Would you rather I asked for someone else to be your liaison officer?" asked Carol, eventually.

Mary shrugged but didn't speak.

"I'm really sorry but I was only doing my job. I do what I'm told and sometimes it isn't nice."

Mary appeared to ignore her as she made no response.

"Look, if we are to continue to work together we are going to have to speak. I know you're hurt but you are going to have to make a decision here. It's your call."

Mary still said nothing. She had withdrawn into herself and barely heard a word Carol said.

Carol looked at her properly and saw a blankness in her dull eyes. Realising for the first time that Mary was present in body but was somewhere else in her mind. Carol went and knelt on the floor beside Mary and put her hand on Mary's arm.

"It's all right Mary. It will be ok. Would you like a cup of tea?" Still nothing.

Carol decided to act and got up to make tea for both of them. By this time she had spent enough time with Mary to know where things were kept in the kitchen. While boiling the kettle she kept an eye on Mary but there was no movement. She sat stiff and upright not displaying any sign that she knew what was going on around her. Carrying two cups of tea through she tried to give one to Mary who didn't take it or even look at it. Carol needing to get the hot, sweet liquid into Mary, held the cup to her lips as if she were a baby. Mary sipped, but still showed no sign of being present in the room. Screwing up her face at the sweet tea Mary withdrew her mouth quickly.

"I know you don't like it but you need something hot and sweet to bring you round. I'm really getting worried about you."

Nothing. Carol held the cup to Mary's mouth again and this time Mary took a few sips which Carol found encouraging. She may not be able to respond but she was at least listening to what Carol said.

When the cup was empty Carol sat on the sofa drinking her own tea, which was getting cold by this time.

"That must be cold now. Why don't you go and make yourself another one," said Mary's voice in a whisper.

Carol jumped, so surprised at hearing Mary's voice. Some of the tea spilt on her trousers when her arm jerked.

"I think I will," responded Carol, deciding it would be a good idea to leave Mary alone for a few minutes.

Back with the tea Carol sat down and sipped the now hot tea.

"I don't want anyone else. I can't bear the thought of anyone else coming and making judgements about me and my Beth."

"I can understand that," said Carol quietly.

"I just want my Beth back. Where is she?"

"I don't know. When we find out who has taken her we'll have a better idea where to look. Are you sure you can't think of anyone who might have a grudge against you who might have taken her?"

"I thought you were thinking it was something to do with Jez and those photos."

Carol shook her head. "There is no suggestion of a link between them anymore. Jez is being held on other grounds but we don't think he had anything to do with the disappearance of your little girl."

"Am I still on the suspect list."

Carol said nothing. She didn't want to upset Mary again but couldn't completely deny it either. Unfortunately Mary picked that thought up from the silence.

"I didn't do it you know. I loved my Beth."

"Maybe you were tired and she was playing up. It would be understandable as a single mum. You have no one to help you and kids can be a handful sometimes."

"My Beth was a good girl she'd never play me up."

"That doesn't sound realistic. All kids play up sometimes. It's normal."

"She didn't. I think it's because she became used to having to behave and be quiet and not bring herself to Jez's attention."

Carol sat up straight, making a mental note of what Mary had just said. It sounded just like she was suggesting something between Jez and Beth.

"What do you mean? Can you be a bit more specific?" asked Carol, treading carefully as she felt they could be on the verge of a breakthrough.

"As I've told you before Jez hated children. He hadn't wanted Beth which is why he eventually moved out. I had to keep Beth out of his way so as not to anger him. He had a filthy temper."

"Did he ever hurt you or Bethany?"

"Not physically. Psychologically was a different matter altogether. He was always telling her how useless she was. Telling her not to talk to him. She was often in tears from his brutal words. She couldn't understand why her daddy didn't want her. When she was with her friends there dads were loving and warm. She often asked what she had done to make him hate her."

Carol's eyes filled with tears and she had to turn away to hide it from Mary. This was the closest they had come to hearing about the family dynamics.

"That's why I don't think Jez could have done this. He wouldn't want Beth around."

"Could he have taken her and hurt her?"

Mary shook her head. "I don't think so. The less he saw of her the better."

Carol found this helpful and felt they could remove Jez from the suspect list. He still had a key though so could Anne Marie have got hold of the key somehow and taken the little girl. If that were the case what motive could there be?

"What about his new partner, Anne Marie, do you think she could have done."

"How?"

"She could have managed to get the key somehow."

"That doesn't make sense. How could she have done it. He would have missed her if she got up in the middle of the night and snuck out to come here. Also she would know of his feelings about children so she wouldn't do that. She's not stupid she must know all of this."

"Hmm."

"You're not sure."

Carol shook her head, "I'm not. It would be interesting to have another chat with our friend Anne Marie. I'm going to make another phone call about this."

Out in the hall with doors shut she made the brief to Adam. Adam got excited and said he'd get straight on to it.

Back in the room with Mary she said, "They are going to question Anne Marie again but they don't really think she had anything to do with it. We are sure Jez will have make his feelings on the subject very clear, especially when Anne Marie would question why he never sees his daughter."

"He could have lied about it to make it my fault in some ways. I don't know."

"That's possible," said Carol. She wasn't convinced though. Anne Marie wasn't stupid, far from it, and was likely to have worked it out for herself.

………

"Why would I want someone else's brat?" asked Anne Marie when Adam phrased the question.

"You have already said you wanted children."

"Yes but my own not someone else's."

"Maybe you thought given Beth you could make him come around to the subject."

"That would never have happened. He got quite cross if ever I brought the subject up."

…………

Carol relayed this back to Mary when she heard from Adam. It seemed Anne Marie was in the clear at least for now.

"It must be someone who knows us," commented Mary, who was starting to feel very frustrated. She felt she wasn't being taken seriously as if the thought was still there that it was down to her.

The phone rang. Mary paled as she heard the voice on the other end. Carol stood up and rushed to her needing to listen as well.

"You….never….learn….do….you," said the robotic voice.

Carol tried to disguise her shock for no one had really believed there was any phone call and robotic voice until now. It had sounded too much like a science fiction story. It changed everything. No way could Mary have made the phone call to herself. She had been sat with Carol when it occurred. This surely meant Mary was in the clear after all.

At the end of the call Carol said, "I'm going to have to call this in."

Coming back into the room she smiled at Mary. Not for anything would she tell Mary the truth about the phone call. Sergeant Macintosh still didn't totally believe it and suggested that Mary could have got someone to make the call while Carol was there just to put them off the scent. He totally believed Mary must be involved in some way.

Carol believed firmly in Mary now. It was going to be difficult to continue to investigate while the sergeant held that view though. He still wanted the focus to be on Mary. Carol and Adam who also believed Mary now were going to have to go it alone somehow, without getting into trouble themselves. Mary would only be in the clear if they found out who was behind it. The main people were not able to have done anything, Mr Stubbs was dead and Jez and Anne Marie were still being held in custody. None of them could possibly have arranged for that phone call to take place.

Whoever it was knew that Carol was still with Mary and didn't want her involved. It suggested that the perpetrator could be watching Mary. Carol didn't like this thought as it could put Mary in danger in some way. There was no way she could stay around twenty four seven but the sergeant wouldn't allow anyone to take over while he thought it was somehow all down to Mary. It was ludicrous to think that, especially in the light of the recent phone call that she had witnessed herself.

Carol decided the best thing was to speak to the sergeant and really state what she had observed.

………

Back at the station she managed to collar the sergeant before he left for the day.

"Look we have to do something about this Mary situation. I am sure she's in danger. The caller knew I was there which suggests Mary is being watched."

"I don't see how. No one has attempted to approach Mary so I doubt the need for caution. What would they gain from watching her? Absolutely nothing. They have already taken Beth so watching Mary sounds all wrong."

"I see your point but we don't know as yet why Bethany was taken so we should take precautions and protect Mary."

The sergeant was getting frustrated. This all seemed completely pointless. "As I have already said it is unnecessary. This seems all about children not the parents."

"But what if Mary knows something about them or may have even seen them?"

"If she had she would have told us."

"That's not guaranteed she is very wary of us. Or maybe she saw something but didn't realise its significance."

The sergeant shook his head, his patience wearing thin now. "I have said it's not needed. How many times do I have to tell you."

Adam hearing the conversation was getting heated decided to take a hand. "Come on Carol let's go. You won't achieve anything here."

Adam and Carol walked off. The latter fuming at the way her thoughts were just dismissed out of hand. The sergeant had his views and nothing would change his mind.

"I want to go back to Mary's. I really think someone needs to be there with her."

"Ok I'll take you. But I'm staying as well."

"You don't need to. I don't want you to get into trouble as well."

"I'm staying and that's final. I believe your instincts. If anything happens you won't have any back up so I will be there with you. I don't want you in danger either."

"Thank you," said Carol who appreciated the offer. It would give her someone to talk to at the very least.

They soon arrived at Mary's house and Carol explained that both of them would be staying the night for a change,

Mary wasn't stupid so asked, "Why two and why overnight. What are you hoping for?"

"We just want to make sure you are safe that's all."

"There has to be more to it than that."

"We're thinking you might have another phone call and we don't want to miss it. If it does happen try and get some information out of the caller or if not maybe stay on the line longer to get something. Even some sort of recognition of who the caller might be."

"I can do that without the two of you being here. One I could maybe believe but both of you. I think you should tell me what's going on as you are frightening me now."

"Ok," said Carol, proceeding to tell her the shortened version. She missed out the bit about no one believing her still. She didn't want to upset Mary more than necessary.

Mary nodded when she heard the story. "That makes sense thank you. I appreciate your honesty as I had the feeling that the sergeant doesn't believe me."

Adam and Carol exchanged brief looks. "He doesn't does he," she said incredulous that the recent phone call in front of Carol hadn't made any difference. She didn't say anything though. She didn't want to hear the truth. If she were in danger as she suspected the two officers would be there to protect her and hopefully catch the person responsible.

During the night Mary got up and wandered downstairs. She jumped when she saw Adam and Carol. She had forgotten they were staying,

The two officers were still awake and talking quietly when Mary appeared. They looked up and Carol said, "Can we get you anything?"

Mary shook her head. "I couldn't sleep. I've been like this since Beth went missing."

Carol nodded in sympathy, "I can understand that."

"I keep hoping she'll turn up in the middle of the night just like she disappeared. Nothing so far."

"We're here to keep vigil so why don't you have a night off patrol duty and get some sleep. That's what's advisable for you."

....

Back at the station the sergeant was asking if anyone had seen the two officers. His smiling face became grim as he heard where they had gone. He had specifically told Carol no! "Let them know I want to see them the minute they get back," he said.

....

Of course the sergeant would take that view. It doesn't fit into his theories does it," said Adam, having taken the phone call from a fellow officer. "We won't be coming back yet."

It was at that moment the phone rang again. Mary looked at it uncertainly until Adam picked it up passed it to Mary with a nod that she should take the call.

"That's….right…..don't….sleep…..we……have…….some…….talking …….to ….do."

Mary paled as she listened to the message. "Who is this?" she asked faintly having no voice for this.

"That's…..for…..me……to…..know…..and…..you…..to…..find…..out.,,,"

"Is Beth ok?"

"Yes."

The phone went dead. It had actually been a shock to the person on the other end of the phone to realise the police were there. That was an unexpected turn up for the books. They didn't know what had made them realise the police were there. There was just something different about Mary's voice and the man's voice as he passed the phone to Mary. Hmm, things were getting more tricky. They had wanted to give Mary a riddle to solve which would hopefully send her on a wild goose chase. The police presence had changed that. Something else would have to be thought of. Aha, the beginnings of an idea. The police couldn't stay indefinitely then time to have some fun!

Mary had a more peaceful night than she'd had in ages, Carol and Adam being there helped. She knew they would answer the door if Beth returned home.

The phone rang. Adam picked it up with a glance at Carol who gave a nod.

"Who…..are……you?
I…..need…..to…..speak……to…..Mary."

"Mary's asleep and I'm not going to wake her. She needs a good night. As for who I am, I'm a police officer and to whom am I talking?"

"Never…..mind…..who…..I…..am….Is…..Mary…..ok…..plea se……tell……her….she…..is….to……go……to……the…..park …..near…..the……..pond……"

"Why?"

"She'll…..find…….out……."

Adam put the phone down and looked at Carol with a concerned look that matched hers. No way were they going to let Mary go alone. It could be too dangerous and after all it was the same place that Mr Stubbs was killed. It couldn't be a coincidence surely.

"I'll go and wake her and let her know."

"Good idea. I better phone the station and let them know in case we need backup."

"Great."

"What do you think you are doing going behind my back? I told the other woman that you were not to put yourselves in that position."

"We have to go. It might be our only chance to see who is behind this."

"You really think they'll bother to turn up, knowing the big possibility they'll be police there. You'll never make a detective if you don't start to think." With this last cutting remark the sergeant put the phone down, wondering where they got their officers from these days. Idiot school maybe, he thought grimly.

Chapter Eighteen

It was three o clock and Mary was stood where she had been told to with her back to the pond exactly as instructed. While she was there Carol and Adam were positioned in bushes ready to charge if need be. The time went on but nobody revealed themselves. In fact the park was completely empty so they couldn't even mistake anyone for the kidnapper. They gave up and went over to Mary.

"Come on, let's go. No one is coming. We've waited an hour now."

"Can't we wait a bit longer?" queried Mary who had decided that was the day the kidnappers would give Beth back.

"No point," said Carol. "Come on. Let's get you home and have a cuppa."

Mary sighed, two solitary tears sliding down her face.

"It's ok, Let it out, it will be good for you."

"I was so sure," sobbed Mary.

"I know. We have seen this happen time and again and usually nothing happens. It's the kidnappers way of playing mind games."

"But why?"

Carol shrugged, "I don't know," she said. "It really depends on who the kidnapper is and their motive for acting in the first place."

"Is Beth likely to still be alive?"

"It again, depends on the motive. We can never give up hope," replied Carol. She was being careful how she answered that one as it would be wrong to take Mary's hope away from her. Experience told her though that the longer it was left the less chance there was of getting Beth back alive.

....

"What now?" asked Mary when they got her back home.

"We have to go back to the station and face the music," said Adam.

"What have you done?" asked Mary.

"Staying here with you. It was frowned upon by the detective sergeant in charge of the case."

"Sorry I didn't mean for you to get into trouble."

"It's not your fault we chose to come. We knew we would be for it when he found out. We can't put it off any longer."

....

"You're back then, my office now."

The two officers meekly followed their sergeant into his office and stood looking down at the ground. They were ready to stand up for their actions though believing themselves to be in the right.

"Ok what have you got to say for yourselves?"

"I felt there was good reason to stay with Mary. There was a possibility she was in danger and I wanted to make sure nothing happened to her. I was justified……" said Carol until she was abruptly stopped by the sergeant putting his hand up.

"You were justified did you say. When is it a good idea to go against the advice of CID? You seem to have got a bit above yourself here."

"But sir she received the robotic phone call again which we both witnessed. She was to go to the park near the pond."

"Hmm, the pond you say. What happened next?"

Carol hung her head as this was the bit that would prove the sergeant right.

"Well, I'm waiting," demanded the sergeant.

"Nothing. We were there as requested but no one turned up. Not even a dog walker in sight."

"This appears to prove my point. Nothing happened. Mary could still have arranged it with a friend. You've said she has a close friend."

"Liz, sir."

"Liz. Have you spoken to her to see what she knows about it."

"No we thought we better come back here. You seemed to want to see us urgently."

"So urgent was it that you left it most of the day before coming."

"We couldn't come sooner as we had to go to the park."

"And you thought I would disapprove of it."

"Well, yes sir."

"And what have you got to say for yourself?" he asked turning to Adam who had so far stayed quiet.

"I was in total support of Carol. I believe she made the right call."

"You did, did you."

"It would serve you both right if I took you off the case as of now."

Carol gasped, horrified at the thought. "But…"

"But nothing. I have every right to do that as you have disobeyed my orders. You seem to be getting a bit above yourselves. I am the DS and you are just constables in uniform. I won't do that however as both of you are still more involved and know more about the case and its complexities than anyone else. Plus Mary trusts you Carol so you are still more likely to get the truth out of her. I think the next step is to go right back to the beginning and look at what we know, which doesn't seem to be a lot as we got side tracked with the paedophile ring which only has vague connections to this case."

"What do you want us to do sir?"

"I want you to sit down over the paperwork and go through it thoroughly and see what we know. It's just possible that going through it systematically we might find something we are missing."

Carol and Adam left the office suitably chastened but at the same time jubilant, feeling they had got off very lightly.

They both sat down with the file open between them.

"Shall we take it half each and go through our own section or look at it all together?" asked Adam.

"I think we might get on better if we look at it together. Two heads are better than one and all that."

In silence to begin with they read through the file . Nothing seemed to leap out at them as they ploughed through it. There wasn't anything strange except the robotic voice on the phone. It did seem unbelievable if they hadn't witnessed it for themselves. It made them believe everything that had happened, right down to the phone call that began it all. This was certainly one very odd case. Possibly the weirdest one they had ever been involved in. There was still a question mark in their minds over whether the paedophile ring had anything to do with the disappearance of little Bethany.

"You know if we could work out how the kidnapper got in we may have solved the case as it could tell us who it was."

"If only," said Carol, although she did agree with Adam.

"I can only go back to the obvious conclusion that it had to be someone with a key," said Adam.

Carol nodded but not enthusiastically. "We came to a grinding halt with that thought didn't we right at the beginning."

"I know but we need to think it through more carefully. Did anyone lose a key even if for a brief time…"

"…long enough for someone to get a key cut," continued Carol starting to smile. "It would give us a new starting point. We need to speak to Mary again about who has a key and then take it from there. Interview them all to see if anyone did notice the key missing."

Adam smiled, "Now we have to go to the sergeant and get the go ahead to approach this line of questioning."

"You can do that, it's your idea after all," said Carol.

"Coward," responded Adam. "Ok I'll go and face the music if he decides to pour scorn on the idea."

Adam wasn't gone long before he returned with a big grin and gave Carol the thumbs up. "He thought it was a brilliant idea."

"Really?"

"Well, maybe that's a bit of an exaggeration but he came round to the idea when I pointed out we had nothing else to go on."

"Well done. Come on let's go before he changes his mind."

They hurriedly left the building, feeling more positive than they had done. At least they knew what they were looking into. It really did make sense in their minds. It had to come down to who had the keys.

Carol stopped abruptly making Adam bump into her as he had been a few steps behind.

"Sorry," he said.

"My fault. I just had a sudden thought. What about Jez, he had a key according to Mary last time and he's in custody now. Shouldn't we have spoken to him first while we were there."

"I hadn't thought of that," admitted Adam. "I think since we are on our way to the car we may as well go to Mary and check with her before paying a visit to anyone else."

"That's fine."

……..

It was a slow journey to Mary's, being rush hour traffic. Carol put the radio on and they sat listening to songs from the 80's.

"Gosh this takes me back a bit," said Adam.

"Does it?"

"Yeah I used to love Wham at the time. I was a teenager. You weren't even born then."

Carol shook her head. "You're showing your age now," she teased.

"I don't care. *Wake me up before you go go….*"

"You even remember the words. I've never heard of the song."

"It was my all time favourite back then."

"This is proving to be an interesting journey," said Carol. "I'm finding out things about you that I never knew."

"Don't go around spreading it about. I'll get teased mercilessly if you do. I've even got all the Wham stuff at home still. All their old records."

"Records? You really are living in a time warp aren't you."

"None of this modern stuff for me," said Adam, knowing he was digging a hole for himself and leaving himself open to more ribbing from Carol and others if the word got out.

"So you've never used MP3s then?"

"What are they?"

"You don't even know. Which century are you in."

"The 20th."

"I can tell. It's about time you came into the 21st."

"Kicking and screaming it will be."

"Well ok if that's what it takes."

"It's about time I took you in hand."

"Oh yeah."

"Yes. Firstly you can have a play on my ipad and see if you can work out how to use it and the apps."

"I might break it though," said Adam reluctantly. He wasn't sure he wanted to get involved with all this modern technology. It was bad enough that he had to learn how to use a computer and email for the job. They often communicated by internal emails these days. Sometimes depending what the case was they needed to look things up on the internet. What had happened to good old pen and paper, he wondered now.

"Here we are. The house is in darkness. Look all the curtains are closed."

"So they are," said Adam, all business like again.

"I hope everything's all right," said Carol. She felt concerned for Mary who never closed the curtains this early always wanting to look outside to see if Beth was coming back.

"Let's knock and hope she answers," said Adam, seriously. He too was picking up the tension that Carol was feeling.

They waited but no one answered their knock. Carol tried again but still nothing. Both were starting to feel anxious now.

"Are you there Mary?" Carol called through the letter box. "It's Carol and Adam. Can you open up."

Nothing, but Carol stood up her brow wrinkled in concern, "I'm sure I heard a noise in there."

"Let me try," said Adam. He bent down and called through the letter box, listening carefully.

"You're right. There is a faint noise, it sounded muffled."

"What shall we do?" asked Carol.

"We'll go around the back and see if we can get in or see something."

They found curtains closed and doors and windows locked.

"I'm calling it in," said Adam. "We need to get in there."

Carol nodded and waited while Adam made the call.

"The serge is sending a squad car out with the permission to break in if necessary."

"You mean he's taking it seriously?" Carol asked in surprise.

Adam nodded. "I must have said something right."

It wasn't long before back up arrived.

"You need to get in?" asked Jeremy, hurrying over to Adam and Carol.

Adam briefly explained the situation.

"Ok we'll take it from there."

Jeremy knelt down, also calling through the letter box. "You're right," he said standing up. "There is someone in there."

He stood aside for colleagues to break open the door. "Be careful," he reminded everyone as Adam and Carol entered.

Carol got out her gloves to open the living room door. They had to be careful as they were aware they could be entering a crime scene. She walked in slowly and quietly, Adam following.

She gasped as she saw Mary tied to a dining room chair with tape over her mouth so she could only make a muffled sound. The other officers seeing this went upstairs quietly in case the perpetrator was still present somewhere.

Carol went straight over to Mary and tore the tape from her mouth.

"Who did this?" asked Carol immediately.

"I don't know," whispered Mary. "Someone came in the back door which I had left stupidly left unlocked. They wore black and a mask over their face. They spoke in that strange robotic sounding voice."

"What did they say?"

"They made it very clear this was my punishment for involving the police. They said they did turn up at the pond but couldn't approach because you were hiding."

"They must have been watching from a distance as there was no sign or sound of anyone."

"They made it clear if I spoke to you again I would never see Beth."

Carol gasped. "I'm so sorry. I have to write all this down and you need to sign the statement."

Carol drew back and had a whispered conversation with Adam. He nodded and left the room.

"Adam's gone to call an ambulance for you and to see what approach we need to take next."

"I don't want an ambulance. I'm fine."

"You maybe but it's my duty to get you checked out and ensure you're ok as a victim of a crime."

"I'm more worried about Beth."

"Adam will sort something out with the sergeant. It's beyond us now. I expect he'll want to come out himself."

"Does he have to. After the way he treated me at the station I don't want to see him."

"Unfortunately he's in charge of the case so he'll probably want to see you himself and do his best to ensure your safety until the case is solved."

Carol didn't say what she was thinking, that it would be looking for a dead child now. With this turn of events that's what they would be doing next as well as interviewing everyone again.

The ambulance arrived at the same time as the sergeant. Mary shrank back when she saw him but he approached slowly and knelt down beside her.

"Well, you've certainly been through a lot," he said gently, not wanting to frighten her into silence. He had seen her withdraw and needed to get her on side.

Mary said nothing.

"Ok, we need to get this lady into the ambulance," said the paramedic.

The sergeant and Carol moved back giving them room to move.

"Is she all right?" asked Carol, feeling concerned.

"Yes, we're just taking her as a precaution. It seems they did nothing but tie her up and threaten her."

"Ok. We'll follow behind and meet you at the hospital," said Carol.

Mary nodded, not sure if she wanted them there but realising she had no choice. She needed to cooperate or it would look as if she had somehow arranged this herself. She couldn't help but think like that after the way she had already been treated by the sergeant. She was very wary. Frightened that they would take her to the station again.

………

Mary was back home with Carol with her overnight with Adam. The sergeant had been surprisingly nice to her and had done everything he could to reassure her he would get it resolved and get Beth back home with her.

There was to be someone with Mary at all times for now to protect her. Carol and Adam were to stay until the morning when they would go and interview everyone who had keys to the house. They knew of course, that the perpetrator had entered through an open door to get to Mary so it didn't have to be someone with a key. The thought was in Carol's mind which hadn't occurred to her before that maybe she had accidentally left a door unlocked that night and that was how the kidnapper had got in.

She needed to put this to Mary but decided to wait until the morning. Mary had been through enough for one day.

They all slept undisturbed that night much to Carol's relief. Part of her had been worried that someone would come back in. This haunted her dreams as she felt responsible in some way. If she hadn't insisted on going to the park and hiding there maybe it wouldn't have happened. If they hadn't left her to go back to the station it would never have happened. She felt she had failed Mary.

Adam sensing what she was thinking said, "You can't blame yourself. It's not your fault. We had to follow orders however much we didn't want to. We had broken enough rules"

Carol shook her head, "I can't accept that. It was still my choice. I could have refused."

"If you had I wouldn't have let you, we were in enough trouble already without heaping more on ourselves. Besides no attempt had been made to get to Mary so it should have been perfectly safe."

Carol nodded, "Maybe," she said, remaining unconvinced.

"You don't believe me do you?" he asked.

Carol shook her head.

"It's true though. If you think about it you'll see that for yourself."

"I can't do that. I should never have let you talk me into going back to the station."

"You didn't really have much choice, besides nothing had happened to Mary at that point and we had no actual evidence that anything would happen."

"I suppose not."

Chapter Nineteen

"Ok Mary we need to go back to the beginning and ask about keys. Who had access to keys? Now that doesn't just mean who had a key but who could have got hold of one," said Carol.

Mary looked puzzled.

"I mean partners, children, absolutely anyone who could have got hold it without anyone knowing."

"Liz has one of course. Her son but he's too young to have done anything. He's only the same age as Beth." Tears came into her eyes as she mentioned her daughter. It had seemed so long without her but in fact it had only been two weeks. It felt more like years.

"You said before that Jez still had one?"

"I think he gave his back when he left. I'm not sure. It's all a jumble in my mind. That's ok we don't need to worry overly much. He was in custody anyway so we know it wasn't him. Anne Marie could have got hold of it couldn't she?"

"His floozy? I suppose so. I wouldn't have thought of that."

"That's why we're asking these questions to get as much information as we can. These extra questions can open up other possibilities."

Mary nodded. "What about Jez's boss?"

"He's not been working for a while. He was sacked remember."

"Would that have stopped him from getting the key if he wanted it?"

"I suppose not. You've got a point there. I'd never have thought of going down that road, but yes we must of course. He knows Jez and the situation so could have had access. Especially if Jez left the keys in a jacket pocket and hung it up out of sight somewhere."

Mary nodded. "I don't know anyone else though."

"That doesn't matter," said Carol. "We'll interview everyone on this list and they'll give us names of others they know who could have had access to their keys. Hopefully this line of questioning will give us a clue as to the way forward or even show us who the kidnapper is."

"What am I going to do while you are doing that?"

"Colleagues will come and sit with you so you'll be fine."

"But I don't know them. How will I know it's not them doing it?"

"It's fine. It will only be people I can trust to give of their best. You won't come to any harm with them sitting with you."

Mary gave a small smile but Carol could tell she wasn't convinced. It wasn't surprising she supposed. They had let her down badly by not believing her in the first place and leaving her vulnerable. There was nothing she could do to persuade her she could just hope that Mary would learn to trust them again. To learn that they had her best interests at heart.

Liz was the first port of call when they left Mary. They knocked but no answer.

"Come on, there's no one in, let's move on and see Anne Marie," said Adam when it was clear no one was going to answer.

Back in the car Carol kept looking across at Liz's house. There was part of her that had a strange feeling about it.

"What is it?" asked Adam.

"I don't know. Just a feeling that's all. "

"A feeling about what?"

"About Liz."

"Surely you don't really believe it's been her all along do you?"

"I'm not sure. Call it intuition, there's just something. I can't put my finger on it at the moment though."

"I trust your intuition. It's usually spot on."

"I know. Look can we have another try and see what happens?"

They approached the house again. This time Carol rang the bell and called through the letter box.

This time they didn't have to wait long before Liz answered. "Yes?" she queried on the doorstep, not wanting to let them in.

"Can we come in? We want to talk to you about Mary?"

"Is she ok? We're not speaking much at the moment, not since that scene."

"We just want to speak about those who have keys."

"You think it's someone who has a key?"

"We're not sure. Just covering all bases really," said Carol being cagey not wanting to give too much away.

"You'd better come in I suppose. Excuse the mess."

They managed to find a space on the sofa to sit. Although the place was certainly cluttered as Liz had intimated.

"You have a key don't you?" asked Carol.

Liz nodded, not saying anything.

"Do you know of anyone else who has a key or could have accessed one from a key holder."

"Was it someone who got hold of a key somehow?"

"We don't know anything for sure. We are looking at every angle possible now."

"Why suddenly? You weren't doing much before except arresting my friend."

"That was a mistake. We were just following orders."

"Yeah, right."

"Look we're sorry about it but we were duty bound to obey orders, but now more information has come to light but we can't divulge what that is," said Carol, pre-empting what she thought Liz would ask next. No way was she going to say anymore. She didn't know why she just didn't trust Liz all of a sudden.

"I don't know anyone else who had a key except Jez of course."

"He's locked up and unlikely to be out in the near future so we know it's not him."

"How can you be so sure. He wasn't locked up then. He would be top of my list being an ex and not liking children. Maybe he and Anne Marie plotted it between them. Or it could have been Mary herself which is what you started to believe if I'm right."

"We can't comment on that I'm afraid."

"Well from what I know only Jez had another key. Anne Marie could have taken it I suppose. No one could have had access to my key."

"How could you be so sure?" asked Adam, speaking for the first time.

"I keep it in my handbag on my key ring along with my keys. They have never left my possession."

Seeing they weren't going to get anymore information out of Liz they stood up to leave.

"I hope you find Beth soon."

"Well we didn't get much from her," said Adam when they were back in the car.

"No I thought she was being very guarded about what she said."

"I agree," said Adam. "I quite saw what you meant about her before we went in. I don't trust her after that."

"Well, we won't get anywhere just sitting here we may as well go and see Anne Marie."

. . . .

They were sitting comfortably enjoying a cup of tea with Anne Marie who had just given them a slice of homemade carrot cake to go along with the tea. Her hospitality really lifted Carol who had been feeling quite down after their visit to Liz. She knew there was something but had no proof of anything as yet.

"Right what can I do for you?" asked Anne Marie while they were busy eating and drinking.

Carol told her what they needed to know.

Anne Marie shook her head bemused. "Sorry I can't help you. I didn't even know Jez still had a key to Mary's place."

"So you never saw an extra key on his keyring then."

"I don't think I even saw the keys. He had quite a number. Actually I had assumed he'd given the keys back to Mary when they broke up."

"Not according to Mary who says he still has a key."

"Well I suppose she would know. I'm surprised she didn't insist she take it back."

"I think she was too stunned by what was happening."

"Well if there is nothing more I can do for you I have a lot to be getting on with. I'm trying to set up my own business."

"Oh what business is that?" queried Carol who was genuinely interested.

"Interior design," said Anne Marie.

"Well good luck with that," said Carol on the doorstep.

"She couldn't wait to see the back of us either," remarked Adam.

"No," said Carol. "We don't seem to be popular with anyone today. "Now we have to go and see Jez's ex boss."

Adam drove off. Driving was slow at this time as people were by now leaving work for the day.

"I'm not sure it's worth it today. We might have already missed him."

"You've got a point. Let's head back to the station."

Turning the car round they followed the route back again.

"At least we haven't had a completely wasted trip," said Adam.

"Not completely. Liz was missing the point. Somehow I got the impression she was hiding something."

"I have to agree with you there. Something was making her very twitchy."

"Thinking back to when Bethany went missing I'm trying to remember how Liz was then," said Carol.

"That's an interesting point actually. I'm not sure I took much notice. My thoughts were on Mary and the missing child. Liz was just a prop in the puzzle, holding Mary afloat."

"I have to agree unfortunately. I think I only started taking notice when she reacted so badly when Mary became convinced that child was her Bethany."

"For me it was when we were with Liz a short while ago. She was behaving oddly and couldn't wait to get rid of us."

"I wouldn't mind having a chat with the sergeant about her, to see what his input is."

Adam agreed with this. Liz certainly needed more attention paid to her. Maybe even a formal interview. At the station she would have no distractions to use as an excuse to get them to leave.

....

"How did you get on?" asked the sergeant.

"We only had time to see Liz and Anne Marie and both of them were in a hurry and couldn't wait to get rid of us," said Carol. "In fact we wanted to talk to you about Liz as she seemed to be acting a bit strange we both thought."

She proceeded to go over the interview with Liz in detail. The sergeant didn't interrupt and used all his listening skills to make sure he got everything and then he could mull it over in his mind and come up with something useful for the next step, if they needed to delve further into Liz.

"What do we know about her background?" he asked when he was sure he had the gist of it.

"Single parent with one son about six years old."

"Is that all. I think we need to look further into her life. Who is the father of her son for instance? Does she still have contact with him? How long has she been friends with Mary?"

"That's interesting. Do you want us to speak to Mary again about her or speak directly to her?"

"Umm, Mary first maybe then we'll reassess the situation. It may be that we won't need to take it further if Mary can satisfy us."

"We can do that tonight when we go back to sleep over."

"Good idea. Then if necessary Liz can be brought in tomorrow."

It was dark by the time they reached Marys but it wasn't a problem as the previous shift would be there waiting. Mary was already in her nightie ready for bed. She had obviously been crying from her tear stained cheeks. Carol felt for her. It must be hard to lose your child and not know if they were alive or dead and if you would ever see them again. Mary seemed so alone now that the friendship with Liz seemed all but over. She hoped Mary would be able to answer the questions that needed to be asked honestly without feeling guilty that she might get Liz into trouble.

"Where have you been?" asked Mary.

"We were interviewing people who had the keys as we said when we left here. On that subject we need to ask you a few more questions about Liz."

"Liz? Why? What has she done?"

"We don't know that she's done anything yet but she was very funny with us and was extremely reluctant to let us in."

"That's not like her. She's usually bubbly and ready for a chat. She's a terrible gossip but a lot of fun as well."

"We certainly didn't see that side of her today. Could it be because the two of you had a falling out?"

"It could be I suppose but I don't think so. It still doesn't sound like her."

Carol and Adam looked at each other. They were both suspicious now, even more so than before. The person Mary was describing didn't fit the Liz they spoke to. Was it really possible Liz was the kidnapper all along and had only pretended to be Mary's friend. Carol was becoming sure in her own mind that this was the case but what was the motive? There appeared to be no motive as yet and the sergeant wouldn't agree to anything much without that. Without a motive they had no grounds to hold her and a solicitor would soon wipe the floor with them.

According to Mary, Liz was a loving, caring person, an extrovert who loved being around people. She was a terrible gossip, loving nothing more than exaggerating anything juicy that she could get her teeth into. Mary didn't know who Simon's father was as that was one subject Liz refused to talk about. She always said it didn't matter, Simon never asked and was quite happy with Liz. Carol couldn't think of any more questions. When she mentioned the possibility of Liz being the guilty one Mary was horrified, absolutely certain that her friend would never do such a thing. If it were her why would she be there for Mary trying to help her through it.

Carol had no answer.

Adam changed the subject, seeing that it was upsetting Mary too much to think like that about her friend. He really hoped for Mary's sake that Liz turned out to be innocent. He hated to think how Mary would react to hearing of her guilt. They spent the rest of the evening chatting and general things and keeping off the case which was good for all of them. They needed a break from it to be able to sift through and work out was relevant.

Carol didn't sleep that well. Not surprising on an uncomfortable sofa with springs that had broken. She lay there still not wanting to find yet another spring that felt as if it was digging into her body. To pass the time she went through everything they knew about the case so far. She was sure they were missing something obvious, that maybe they had everything they needed to crack the case. While they had been focussed on Mary because there was no break in they had been missing other clues. She was sure she had the answer in her mind. She couldn't wait until morning to go over it with Adam to see what he thought and then discuss with the sergeant.

Carol didn't have to wait long as Adam, who was sleeping in Beth's room, much to Mary's annoyance, couldn't sleep either and went downstairs.

"You're awake as well," she said.

Adam nodded, "I keep going over everything in my mind and can't switch off."

"Same here and I think I've got the solution. If I'm right I know where Beth is and who has taken her. I even think I know why."

"Really?"

"I don't know how I've come to this conclusion but I have. We haven't even looked in that direction. The key would have been easily to hand as well from two people."

"Come on then, don't keep me in suspense."

Carol outlined her thoughts which seemed to fit together. All the pieces of the puzzle made sense. Adam started to get excited.

"Do we have to wait until morning? Can't we just ring now and get to work. At least everyone will be home and easy to question and search."

"You can try but I don't know how the sergeant will react."

"True," said Adam, trying to kerb his enthusiasm.

They spent the rest of the night talking. In those long hours not only were they talking about the case but about each other as well. Although they had worked together for along time they didn't know each other well. They found common ground between them and grew closer together with a mutual respect and trust.

They were brought to a halt when Mary joined them, yawning. Carol looked at her watch and was surprised to see it was seven. Carol excused herself to go and ring the station. They had agreed not to tell Mary anything until they had the proof and hopefully Beth back at home safe and well. If Carol was right then Beth was never in any danger.

Carol went back in her eyes sparkling. She gave a brief nod to Adam to let him know everything was going ahead with their plan.

"We have to get going Mary. Something's come up. There will be someone here within half an hour. The sergeant has agreed to let us go now as we have some leads to follow up. We'll explain later. We'll make sure all doors are locked before we go. Do not open the door unless it's the police."

Chapter Twenty

Knocking on the door Carol and Adam waited for a reply. "Surely there is still someone in. He can't have gone to work yet," said Carol.

They were about to give up when Matthew answered the door. "Yes?" he queried.

"Hello, I don't know if you remember….." began Adam.

"Yes I do. Is this to do with Jez again? I have nothing more to add from last time." Matthew sounded irritated at seeing them again.

Carol thought for one awful moment that she'd got it terribly wrong. She noticed a brief hardening in his eyes and was sure she was right after all.

"Jez lost his key recently and we thought you might know about it," said Adam.

"Me? How can I know about it. I haven't seen Jez since I fired him."

"Are you sure about that?"

"Of course I am. I'm not senile you know," said Matthew.

"It's all right. There is no need to take that tone with us. We're only trying to get at the truth and return a little girl to her mother where she belongs."

"I realise that but I can't help you. Now if that's all I have to get to work."

"Not so fast. Can I see all your keys please."

Matthew sighed and seeing nothing for it took the bunch of keys out of his pocket.

"We need you to tell us where each one fits then we are going to try them to make sure."

"I'm sick of this, you have no right to barge in here with these ludicrous statements."

"I think you'll find we have. If you don't believe us we can call the sergeant dealing with the case and he can come and speak to you himself. I can assure you he'll bring a search warrant with him."

"Ok, ok. If you must."

Slowly they went through most of the keys. When opening a door to the loft they had a quick look just to reassure themselves that Beth wasn't there. They weren't surprised not really expecting to find her there. No she was most likely being looked after by a woman.

"We'll have to take you to work now so we can test those doors. We can't let you go alone as that will give you time to dispose of any unwanted keys."

Matthew shook his head. "I don't know what you're expecting to find, but it isn't here or there."

"I don't expect it is. You wouldn't be that stupid, you're an intelligent man. You could still have keys that are not accounted for though."

Arriving at Matthew's office they tried the latest key and found it working. They stepped inside glad that no one had arrived yet.

"Ok what is this key for?"

"My drawer. No, before you ask I can't let you look. It contains sensitive information about my clients.

"That's ok you open it, we don't need to look through private documents – at least not yet."

"Not ever!" stated Matthew with certainty.

Sure enough the key worked. Now there were only two keys left. These were the two that interested the two officers. They couldn't see what else Matthew could possibly have a key to.

"Well, we now have two keys left."

"That must be an old key for somewhere," he said pointing to one of the keys. "I can't remember where. The other one belongs to my girlfriend's house."

"We are going to need the name and address of your girlfriend so we can check it out."

"Is that really necessary. I mean, she doesn't even know Jez or Mary."

"We'll be the judge of what's needed and what isn't. We can't take your word for it we need to prove it. That is what the law is all about."

"Yeah, but how has that anything to do with me? I haven't broken the law. I'm sorry for Jez and Mary of course I am, who wouldn't be. But it's nothing to do with me."

"We can't just take your word for it," said Adam.

"I'm sorry I haven't the time now. I have a meeting with a client at ten."

"And I'm sorry but you have to come with us. This is a serious matter and needs taking care of now. Your client will have to wait.

"You don't underst……"

"And you don't understand. If you don't come voluntarily we will arrest you and take you to the station."

"You can't do that I haven't done anything wrong."

"You are getting in the way of our investigation and preventing us from doing our job."

Matthew sighed, "I can see you are giving me no choice. Can I at least ring and get my secretary to put off that meeting?"

"If you give us the number we'll do that for you."

"What is going on here? Am I being accused of something?"

"No one has said that, but we don't want you contacting your girlfriend to warn her."

"Ok come on then. She won't be happy to have the police turn up though. I hope you don't wreck my relationship. She's the one good thing to happen in my life."

"I understand sir but we are just doing our job. After all a small child is missing."

"I still don't see how this affects me, other than by being acquainted with Jez that is."

Finally they persuaded Matthew to get in the car, reminding him that all this time taken up with arguing was going to make him even later for work. Adam drove in silence. Matthew having gone quiet.

Matthew directed them into a small side street where they pulled up. He led them down an alleyway suitable for walking only. They stopped at a door. Adam knocked but got no answer. He tried again but nothing.

"Are you sure about this?" asked Carol as they stood there.

Matthew nodded. "I don't know where she is. She must have gone out early."

Carol and Adam were suspicious, they both felt they were being led on a wild goose chase. It didn't even look the sort of place where any girlfriend of his would live. It was a rundown area and this house was no different. The outside was grubby and needed a coat or two of paint which was currently peeling. There was rubbish everywhere and the small patch of grass that wasn't even big enough to call a garden was overgrown.

Adam with a brief nod from Carol decided to confront Matthew. "Are you sure this is where she lives? What is her full name?"

"Amanda Squires," responded Matthew.

Carol moved a few feet apart and called it in to the station. She waited while they did a check and gave her the results.

Moving back she said, "There is no Amanda Squires at this address. It is the home of a known criminal who is currently residing at her majesty's prison. The house is known to be empty for another month."

Matthew coloured as well he might being caught out in a lie. "I'm not lying I dropped her off here last week and saw her go inside this address."

"Have you ever been inside?" asked Adam.

Matthew reluctantly shook his head. He had thought it strange he'd never been asked back but had just thought she was ashamed of where she lived.

"I think you are either lying or you have been lied to," said Adam.

"She must have lied to me. I swear I'm telling the truth."

"Ok," sighed Carol. "We'll let you go this time but if we find out you've been lying to us we know where to find you."

"I hope you're going to drop me home to pick up my car."

"Of course."

………

"What did you think of that wild goose chase?" Adam asked Carol.

"I think it was just that. He knew exactly what he was doing. He's not stupid. He did well to think on his feet though I'll give him that."

Adam nodded. "What now?" he asked.

"Liz, I think."

"Just check with the station to see if the search warrant is ready first. We don't want another waste of time."

"We certainly don't."

"Ok we're on," said Carol. "We just have to stop off for the piece of paper then we can get going."

They knocked at Liz's door, faces set sternly. This was what they were always heading towards. Carol was certain her theory was right they just needed the proof. They waited and waited but no answer. She couldn't be long surely, not if they were right that was.

"Come on, we're wasting our time, she's not in."

"Or pretending she's not."

"Why would she do that she doesn't know what we suspect."

"She could have heard from Matthew. That was probably stupid of us to let him out of our sight giving him time to alert her."

"He can't have done," said Adam, holding up a mobile phone triumphantly. "I deliberately forgot to give it back to him."

"Good work," grinned Carol.

"I'm surprised we haven't heard about it yet. I expected him to go to the station to complain we didn't give him it back."

"Maybe he hasn't realised yet."

"I can't see that somehow. But it's in our favour anyway."

Carol's phone rang. "Maybe this is it," she said.

She listened responded and disconnected the call. She looked at Adam, face very pale.

"What is it?" asked Adam, very concerned.

"Mary. We need to get there quickly."

Chapter Twenty one

Siren blaring they raced their way to Mary's. Carol hadn't spoken more than that but it was enough. Adam knew there was a serious problem he didn't need to know more.

Pulling up outside they had barely stopped before Carol got out of the car and rushed to the other officers already there.

"She didn't answer the door when we arrived," one said.

"Did you look around the back?"

The officer nodded, saying, "All curtains closed."

"We'll try and get in," said Adam, fast approaching.

Somehow they managed to prise open the patio doors and crept in quietly, not wanting to alert anyone to their presence. What they saw made them rapidly withdraw. There was Mary tied to a chair and behind her stood a person dressed all in black. Including hair covered.

They went back out and whispered to the officers present what they had seen. The station was contacted and the sergeant himself was going to turn up as soon as possible.

During a conflab when he arrived it was agreed he would go to the door and call in to the person keeping Mary captive. Adam and Carol were to stay behind him ready to rush to Mary if the situation allowed.

"Hello, I'm Sergeant Macintosh. Can we have a chat?"

"We have nothing to talk about. I've said everything that needs saying already. Mary is unable to tell you though. She's a bit tied up." The person laughed.

It was impossible to tell if it was male or female as the voice sounded disguised.

Carol taking a giant leap into the unknown, wanted to test her theory. With a nod from the sergeant she stepped in front of him.

"It must be hard Liz….." she said nothing more as the person gasped and turned around.

"H…how did you know?"

"It seemed the most likely outcome. You had pretty much given yourself away with all that you have said to Mary. I was just a bit slow catching up. You were quite harsh to her and no friend would be like that towards Mary's situation."

"I thought I'd been so clever."

While Liz had her eye on Carol, Adam and the sergeant crept in to try and get to Mary.

"No you don't," cried out Liz seeing what they were doing. "I'll cut her throat if you come a step nearer."

"You don't really want to do that. Think of Bethany, how would she feel knowing her mum had been killed?"

"She won't know. She'll forget her and call me and my partner mum and dad."

"So you're admitting you know where she is."

Liz said nothing, realising she'd said too much. She'd been caught well and truly.

"You may as well tell us where she is and if she's all right."

"She's with my partner at the moment. She had been staying with me but we moved her. We have moved her back and forth every few days just in case you started getting suspicious."

"We were a bit slow then as we only worked it out last night."

"I did something right then," said Liz.

Now that she had been identified she took her mask off her face. It was a relief to do so as it made her so hot and itchy.

"Ok are you going to tell us who your boyfriend is and where we can find him. Whose idea was it to take her and for what reason. We'll find out anyway so you may as well tell us the truth."

"I'm not saying anything without a solicitor present."

From that moment they got nothing more out of her. They arrested her and took her to the station where they booked her in and waited for the duty solicitor to arrive.

It was almost evening when a solicitor finally appeared much to everyone's relief. It had been a long wait and they still needed to know where Bethany was which was their first priority. Liz had refused to say anymore on the subject. She knew it was all over for her but wanted to give her boyfriend time to get out if he heard about her arrest.

………

"Where is Bethany?" asked Carol, needing to get straight to the point.

"No comment," said Liz sullen now she had been caught.

"Come on you should tell us. She's a young child. She needs her mum. If she's on her own she'll need food and drink urgently."

"How do you know she's still alive?"

"So you can talk then. Where is she? Then we can get to her quickly."

"Boyfriend."

"Where can we find him?"

"At home unless he's done a runner."

"Name and address please."

"Why should I give it to you?"

"You don't want that little girl to come to harm do you. You have a child of your own so you know how Mary will feel if anything happens to her Beth."

"Don't care. She doesn't deserve a child now she's on her own. No child should grow up without both parents around."

"You're on your own."

"I have a boyfriend and we are going to get married soon."

"Who is he?"

"You've spoken to him so you should know."

Carol was silent for a moment, thinking, who had they spoken to other than Jez, Mr Stubbs and Matthew? It couldn't be the first two so it must be Matthew. She stood up rapidly and left the room without a word. She needed to get officers around there straight away.

"It's Matthew," she said to the sergeant.

"You and Adam get round there now, back up will follow."

………

"We should wait for back up," said Adam.

"I don't think we have time. We need to get Beth now."

"If she's still here. Matthew could well have moved her."

"I know."

It was five minutes to wait before backup arrived. It had seemed like hours for the couple waiting to get in. They were surprised to see Liz in the back of the car.

Carol raised her eyebrows and one of the officers said, "Sergeant Macintosh thought it a good idea. He thought Liz would be able to help in case he gets difficult as Liz will know where Bethany is."

Carol nodded and said no more. She wasn't sure it was a good idea. Liz might be able to communicate with Matthew in some way.

After a rapid knock at the door and no response one of the officers forced their way in. Carol and Adam rushed in first and were surprised to see Matthew sat there quite calm in the living room.

"Why didn't you open up when you heard us?"

"Didn't feel like it," he shrugged.

"Come on you might as well give up and tell us where Bethany is."

"Don't see why I should."

"Matthew it's over. We can't get away with it now. They know everything," said Liz.

"You mean you blabbed," he said his voice full of contempt.

Liz shook her head. "They guessed."

Matthew put his hand in his pocket and pulled out a gun. This was the last thing they expected from a respectable business man.

"Don't make things worse for yourself," said Adam.

"Matthew!" cried Liz, "Put it down."

Matthew ignored her saying, "Don't come any closer or I'll shoot her."

"Matthew that wasn't part of the plan. No one was supposed to get hurt."

Carol and Adam looked at each other, but stayed out of it. Liz was obviously sensible and was more capable of communicating with Matthew now.

"Things changed," he said.

"How? If you shoot now we won't have Beth."

"We won't have Beth now anyway because the police are involved."

"True."

………

Silence reigned for a few minutes. Carol and Adam let it continue to give Liz and Matthew time to think.

"Why don't you tell us where she is?" asked Carol in a calm, quiet voice when she felt the silence had been going on for too long. She felt it necessary to step in as Liz seemed to come to a halt.

"Come on," said Adam, turning to the other officers, "Let's search the place thoroughly. There must be a loft or basement as we searched thoroughly before and found no sign that a small child had even been here.

"You won't find her here," said Liz. "He doesn't keep her here. We thought that would be too close for comfort."

"Where then, Come on Liz you know time is of the essence here. In some part of you there is love for that little girl and for Mary."

"Mary, she's just a whinger. Always moaning about something. Beth is better off without her."

Carol was shocked at this statement. She really had assumed there was a friendship there. Liz had certainly hidden her feelings well.

"I only pretended to be her friend because of Beth."

"Where is she?" asked Carol in a quiet voice. "Come on Liz we've got you anyway so give in and tell us."

"Matthew has a garage a couple of streets away. Inside is a wall about half way down. If you know where to look there is a device which will open it."

"Don't say anymore, I'm warning you," said Matthew pointing the gun firmly at Liz.

"How could you threaten me when you love me?"

"Love? Who said anything about love? It was your fault. You thought it would be a good idea to take Beth. You said you couldn't have anymore children."

Liz crumpled in a heap on the floor.

"That's right you cry, you'll get no sympathy from me. I doubt very much you will in court either."

"How could you be so cruel."

"Why not."

"I wish I'd never met you."

Matthew shrugged and pulled the trigger. Liz sat in shock before falling sideways eyes staring straight ahead with a blank expression. Blood trickled out of her right ear and the side of her mouth.

Adam knelt down but gave a slight shake of his head to Carol. Liz was dead. Shot by her lover for giving them away.

Adam went outside and called for back up immediately. He quickly explained the situation, needing Matthew to stay alive to show them where the garage was and how to get the wall open.

It wasn't long before more officers appeared, but they were unnecessary. Matthew had dropped the gun and fallen to his knees next to Liz and was cradling her head in his hands.

"Come on," said Carol gently, "There is nothing more you can do for her but you can help Beth."

Matthew looked up, defeat written on his face and nodded. Adam and Carol helped him to his feet and they left the house.

In the car he directed them to his garage and they got out. They watched as he went inside and opened the wall with a small lever on the left hand side. It opened slowly and revealed Beth sitting in a chair tied to it with tape over her mouth. Carol rushed to her and rapidly untied her. Beth shrank away obviously frightened by the appearance of more strangers.

"It's ok," said Carol. "We're the police and we're going to take you back to your mummy."

"Mummy," said Bethany in a small voice.

"Yes," said Carol.

"They said she was dead and I'd never see her again." Tears filled the little girl's eyes as she thought of it.

"She's not dead. She has missed you though. She'll be happy to see you."

Beth was too overcome to respond just sat there thumb in her mouth. Her only source of comfort.

Adam went over and whispered something in Carol's ear.

Carol smiled and turned again to Beth, "Your mummy is on her way here. Two more policemen are bringing her here."

It was only five minutes before the car drew up outside and Mary walked in, a look of wonder on her face. As soon as she spotted Beth she ran forwards and picked up the little girl and kissed her all over her face and held her tight, unable to say a word.

Carol watched with tears running freely down her face. She was so happy that this case had ended well, so many involving missing children didn't.

www.ingramcontent.com/pod-product-compliance
Lightning Source LLC
Chambersburg PA
CBHW032010050726
47590CB00006B/2114